A NOVEL

ADRIAN BARNES

TITAN BOOKS

Nod
Print edition ISBN: 9781783298228
E-book edition ISBN: 9781783298235

Published by Titan Books
A division of Titan Publishing Group Ltd
144 Southwark St, London SE1 0UP

First Titan Books edition: September 2015
6 8 10 9 7 5

A CIP catalogue record for this title is available from the British Library.

Printed and bound in Great Britain by CPI Group (UK) Ltd.

All sub-headings taken from Brewer, *The Dictionary of Phrase and Fable*.
Reprinted in 1993 by Wordsworth Editions. Originally published in 1894.

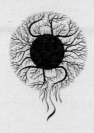

And Cain went out from the face of the Lorde and
dwelt in the lande Nod on the east syde of Eden.

GENESIS

Adam and his race are a dream of mortal mind,
because Cain went to live in the Land of Nod, the
land of dreams and illusions.

MARY BAKER EDDY,
SCIENCE AND HEALTH

Wynken and Blynken are two little eyes,
And Nod is a little head,
And the wooden shoe that sailed the skies
Is a wee one's trundle-bed;
So shut your eyes while Mother sings
Of wonderful sights that be,
And you shall see the beautiful things
As you rock on the misty sea

EUGENE FIELD

For Ethan and Liam

DAY 18
WORDS

The object of words is to conceal thoughts.

It's getting harder and harder to tell the living from the dead.

Most of the remaining Awakened lay sprawled on the asphalt of Birchin Lane, six storeys below my balcony. Down there, everything's akimbo: heads flop, tongues loll, and mouths are corkscrewed holes. Some are still ambulatory and stagger around in unsprung circles, clawing air. Others sit mannequin-still among the rubble, staring up at me from their laps, eyes blazing.

They sacrificed another Sleeper last night, some poor chump in Birkenstocks who's now lashed to a lamp post across the street by bloodstained bungee cords. The head, as always, has been painted lollipop yellow.

And speaking of colours, there's no sign of the Admiral of the Blue this evening: his rickety stage, cobbled together from smashed-down doors and thrashed trash cans, is bare. For a while the Admiral and his people treated me like a prophet, but I always knew it wouldn't last. It's Prophets-R-Us down there: what's in desperate short supply is disciples. It reminds me of poets, before all this—how the sensitive souls who submitted their work to literary journals outnumbered those who read those same publications by a margin of about ten to one. Everyone wanting to be heard; no one interested in listening. Some things never change. Maybe nothing's really changed.

What else do I see? Packs of dogs, heads hovering low, roam the periphery of things. The long-standing human-canine alliance has been irretrievably severed, I'm sincerely sorry to report—the gnawed bones and matted chunks of hair scattered along the shores of Lost Lagoon testify to this. It's sad, but then again those plump collies and German shepherds don't seem too weighed down by nostalgia for bone-shaped vegan treats and belly rubs from the opposably-thumbed as they wander about, licking their chops. Anyway, it's not their fault. We're the ones who broke the deal.

The Awakened spot me, and the crowd's insect noise ratchets up. Beetlemania! I raise my arms, just for old time's sake, and the street falls silent. I hold the pose for a moment then let them drop—a cue for the haunted house screaming to begin.

I'm sure this all sounds pretty terrible, dear hypothetical reader, but you might be surprised to learn that I'm of the opinion that while things are bad now, they really weren't much better before. All that's different here in Nod is that the molten planetary core of pain that used to roil away behind our placid smiles has now blurped out into open air. How we used to fetishize and differentiate our feelings. Rage! Hatred! Hunger! Pride! Jealousy! Ambition! Lust! We had a name for everything. But that colourful cavalcade of emotions was just a sham. It was all pain—all of it—all along. Rage was pain, hate was pain, pride was pain, lust was pain. All that's different now is that where pain used to have the luxury of being a bit of a drama queen and playing dress up, now it stands out there on the corner of Birchin Lane, quivering and naked.

And what about Love—our alpha and omega, our porn and our purity? In the past we'd held love in reserve as something special and untouchable, an element of our personal narratives that we felt would, in a pinch, absolve us of all our other petty sins. A Get Out Of Jail Free card, I suppose. But as it turns out, love doesn't set us free—love keeps standing outside the jail on an endless candlelight vigil. So love? Yes, love was pain as well. Especially love.

And so logically then, the question arises: what *isn't* pain?

I stand there on my balcony as the question rises, coiling into the sky above Vancouver, and hangs still, with no breath of breeze to make it blow away. The orange sun, made hazy and huge by the million square kilometre dust cloud that used to be Seattle, is slowly sinking into English Bay. I can almost hear hissing as the day, maybe the last day, extinguishes itself.

Directly across the street from my apartment, in Demon Park, a siege of great blue herons bobs on overburdened cedar boughs. The names we give gatherings of birds are telling: murders of crows, sieges of herons, *unkindnesses* of ravens. They must have made our ancestors nervous. Birds pick at bones and lap at eye juice. Maybe they reminded our forbears that they'd be bones themselves, soon enough. The sight of pigeons waddling along the pavement has always seemed eerie to me; I've never been able to get over all that armlessness.

Behind me, the stairwells gag on fifty apartments' worth of furniture: everything but the kitchen sinks. The building's risen bile cost me a couple of days of heavy labour, but it also bought Zoe and me some time. Since yesterday morning, though, I've been hearing ripping and snapping sounds coming from the lower floors. I'm pretty sure that Blemmyes are burrowing up toward us. White moles, digging into ceilings, discovering floors. Escheresque. Three floors below now? Two?

And speaking of Escher, it's worth recording this for posterity: the artists were right, literally right, all along. Beneath what we used to call 'reality' there was always an Escheresque, a Boschian, a Munchian *fact*—a scuttling Guernicopia of horrors just waiting to be discovered once the civilizational rock was finally overturned. Who'd have thought that the real high wire act of imagining was the *old* world, that seemingly bland assemblage of malls and media that came to a crashing end less than one month ago? Who'd have thought that the real fantasists were the Starbuckling baristas, the school teachers, and the pizza delivery boys? If we'd really stopped and thought, it would have been obvious. A cursory look at the latest appeal from sub-Saharan Africa should have told us that our privileged world was a pretty slapdash affair, always smouldering at the edges.

But no one stopped, and no one thought.

Christ, I'm tired in a million ways. We've been staring into the whites of each other's eyes for weeks now, the Awakened and I—all of us coming up blank. But that's okay. I really don't mind. I'm just about ready to give it all up anyway.

But what about poor, silent Zoë, already asleep in the spare bedroom, curled up with the stuffed grizzly that Tanya gave her? I may be about done with the whole sorry human comedy, but I still want her to survive. I want something that Tanya loved to live on. But tell that to those flayed faces down there, freshly-arrived for the night shift, insomniac suns thrust deep inside their pockets, scorching their thighs.

What about Zoe? What about the *child*?

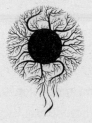

DAY 1
XERXES' TEARS

When Xerxes, King of Persia, reviewed his magnificent and
enormous army before starting for Greece, he wept at the thought
of the slaughter about to take place.

That first morning I was reading about another child—a news story about a boy who ran and ran. 'Incredibly Motivated Kid Takes Flight!' hollered the headline. A breathless tale of how some urchin in San Francisco fled his broken mother, stole a car, outran the cops, made it to the airport, appended himself to a strange family, boarded a plane, and then got himself busted on the other end in LA as he scoured an airport phone book for evidence of his long-done daddy. The kicker? The boy was ten.

It brought tears to my eyes, though I don't know why. When things really move us we never know why, not really. I do remember loving that 'incredibly', though—thought it wonderful that the headline writer's enthusiasm had managed to poke its snout through stale newsprint and sniff my air. A 'kid', not a 'child'. And note that exclamation mark! The headline alone was a masterpiece. I imagined some late night editor leaning back in an empty newsroom and contemplating her handiwork with a wry smile.

The piece didn't have a real ending. It just stopped dead, as news stories do, when the action tank ran dry. The truth was that, beyond story, beyond my flickering interest, that boy was still out there somewhere, enmeshed in some sort of 'care', trapped in Eternal Denouement.

Tanya materialized in the kitchen doorway and pulled me from my daydream.

'Morning.'

'Hey.'

I got up and went over to her. My first thought was that she looked like hell, but I had it backwards. Tanya was heaven; I just didn't appreciate it often enough back then. But my blindness was nothing unusual—in fact, it was almost a good working definition of what it meant to be human. I did know she hadn't slept because she'd kept me up half the night with her sighing and quilt yanking. Now, wrapped in dawn, her warped sheets of hair and the bruise-like black beneath her eyes made her seem both innocent and debauched—a silent child over-filled with knowing. She leaned against the doorway in her nightie—such a strange word, like 'panties'—watching me, leggies not quite directly beneath her torso. Torso. There's no infantilizing that word.

She came over and we kissed with pre-brushing tentativeness, brought together by soft intakes of air, by care. Her hair brushed against my cheek. Hair—she had sheets and sheets of it. Auburn hair that never stayed put. When she pinned it up, it flopped down, when she combed it straight, it curled and twisted. My nickname for her was Medusa.

'I didn't sleep a wink,' she yawned.

'No kidding. It seemed like you were up half the night.'

'Half a night's sleep would have been amazing. It was really fucking weird. I didn't even feel sleepy.'

And it *was* weird. Tanya always slept like a fallen tree in a silent forest, invisible beneath an Oregon of quilts. One sharp little fart every few months—that was about all you'd hear from her between the hours of eleven and seven.

'Too much coffee?'

She laughed. 'Don't you remember? I actually had some warm milk while we watched *Mad Men*. Well, I'll be queen bitch at work today, that's for sure.'

'I had a bad night, too.'

'Poor baby.'

This from someplace inside her distraction. A night watchman or Maytag repairman somewhere inside her scraped brain was looking out for me. And that was love.

I'd slept badly and had a strange dream of golden light seen by something other than eyes. It was still with me there in the morning. Not a shadowy memory, but a vivid one that made the waking world seem drowsy.

'I need a shower.'

She turned and walked out of the room. I watched her go with a miser's attention. Each remembered detail of her face and body was and is precious to me: the curve of her hips, her thin upper lip and full lower one. Even her almost-non-existent earlobes. Sometimes she claimed to be an alien spy, her human disguise flawed only in the earlobe department. She'd confess this to me, then wink.

When Tanya returned, she was freshly laundered and professed herself human. She nuzzled my stubble and guzzled my neglected coffee while I soliloquized on the Incredibly Motivated Kid.

'That's so sad.' She shook her head, sorry for the boy in an uncomplicated way that I could only envy.

Then she dressed in a grey skirt and white blouse and left for work for the last time. Looking back now, I marvel at people who dared wear white. Did they think that the world wouldn't touch them?

Tanya went out, and I stayed in.

In an age when pretty much everyone went out and shook the world's hand all day long, shook it until their hands went numb, their hair turned grey, and their hearts coughed and sputtered, I stayed home and wrote books. On *etymology*, if you can believe that. I know, I know! A great word, etymology. It was a real can of mace when I found myself being nosed at by strangers at parties or on buses: *I write books on etymology.* Watch them stagger, see them scatter—even if ninety percent of them thought that I studied bugs, not the secret origins of words.

My agent, still unsure about me after seven years of contractual bondage, was always pushing for an *Eats Shoots and Leaves* sort of mass placebo, the idea being to try to trick the public into consuming something inherently dry and bland by dusting it with MSG. I never delivered that book. I never refused, mind you—just went ahead and wrote *other* books which, published through unambitious presses, sold just enough copies to shut-ins and fuzzy-sweatered fussbudgets to draw forth more grudging grants, more painful teaching gigs, and to continue the damp seepage of royalties into my checking account.

Our apartment was silly-small; French doors opening onto a one foot deep balcony took up the whole exterior wall of our living room—a failure's balcony that at times seemed to urge me toward a laughable leap. Inside, our home was white and very bright. Behind the living room a kitchenette, and huddled behind that a bedroomette and a bathroomette stocked with lots of tiny soaps and shampoo bottles we'd pilfered from various hotels.

I was working on my latest project that day—a book about the history of sidetracked words, of orphaned and deformed words. An etymological freak show. I was thinking of calling it *Nod*.

Nod. Biblically, it's the barren nightmare land where Cain was sent when expelled from Adam's domain, but at the same time it's a fairy tale kingdom toward which parents urge sleepy children with gentle pressure on the backs of their warm mammalian heads.

Ah, sleep.

In sleep we all die, every one of us, every day. Why wasn't that fact noted more often? When we doze off each night there's never the slightest guarantee that we'll wake the next morning. Every little cat nap is a potential game-ender. So why fear death when we're happy and even eager to make that leap of faith each and every night of our lives? Nod.

Anyway, in forgetting words, my thesis went, we abandon them. But the realities those banished words gave voice to don't vanish: old, unmanned realities lurk eternally in dark woods, in nursery tales, police reports, and skittish memories. Like Grimm wolves.

All the old, whispered words still exist—fantastic words and phrases like 'babies in the eyes', 'cavalry clover', 'doomrings', 'mawworm' 'Blemmye'. Thousands and thousands of them. And when we hear those words, even in the antiseptic light of the twenty-first century, we feel a slight breeze, a chill presence we can't quite identify.

'Birchin Lane' was one phrase I remember wrangling with that day. 'To whip', as with a switch of birch. 'I'm afraid I must take you on a trip down Birchin Lane'. An upper class British accent, the calm dignity before a storm of violence—physical or emotional. We all see this in our loved ones' eyes at some point: the veil about to be torn down.

Untold millions of people have lived on Birchin Lane. Centuries of women and children and not a few men have run the gauntlet down its cobblestone streets. With *Nod*, I was trying to corral Birchin Lane back inside the language, trying to coax it forward in time. The running of gauntlets, the paddling of asses. Cans of whup-ass. Samuel L. Jackson's character speaking so calmly in *Pulp Fiction*: 'I'm gonna get medieval on your ass'. Ass, ass, ass. I considered Guantanamo Bay and Dick Cheney's snigger-smile; I pondered the gym-toned celebrities who fell beneath the media's lash. And the throngs of voyeurs, the millions and millions of people just watching it all. Paris guillotines. Gaza. Damascus.

You'll laugh, but I secretly felt that *Nod* actually had some commercial potential, that people might actually want me to make these sorts of connections for them.

Anyway, working at home, alone, suited me and I seemed to suit it. I didn't have a lot of time for people; you could say I had my reservations about the species. Maybe I'd spent too much time in the forest of unspoken words to emerge with any confidence in my fellow man. Tanya, who had no time for lumbering words like 'misanthropic', elected to believe I was just shy. She was always bringing people by the apartment, beaming friend-candidates for me to assess in the light of her belief I'd find value in them and vote to keep them around. It didn't happen too often, but I'm glad she was wrong about me. And anyway, I loved *her*. Surely that counted for something.

That was the see-saw balance we maintained, face to face, while the world rose and fell in the background. So long as my eyes remained fixed on Tanya's, I never got too seasick. That was the trick.

And so I stayed home and worked all day, never straying far

from the clickity clack, phone and Internet on lockdown so that I could focus and make some solid progress. Every hour or two I'd pause, glance out the window, and there would be the sun, a couple of notches further advanced in its cause, frozen and guilty in the sky.

Tanya got home around five o'clock, just as the sun began staring down its nose at the city. She straight-armed through the door and marched right up to me, stopped, and planted her hands on her hips.

'Have you heard?'

'Heard what?' I asked, pulling most of my face up from the laptop. She'd been warning me lately about half-faces and third-faces, so I was trying to be at least three quarters there for her.

'About last *night*?'

The ascending intonation, the short, stuttering head shake that pantomimes incredulity at another's bone ignorance. I'll call it a 'duh'. Tanya duh-ed me.

'What about last night?'

She began to pace a disgusted circle. I'd been sorting invoices and receipts on the coffee table and as she strode past, the flimsy pieces of register paper trembled in her wake. I saw a fresh coffee stain on her white blouse. Heated by her body warmth, I could actually smell those molecules of connection as she passed my chair, could hear the erotic swish of nylon as her thighs scissored by.

'No one slept, Paul! No one I talked to slept a wink last night.

It wasn't just you and me. Didn't you go out? Didn't you even check the fucking news online?'

'I was—'

'It's all over everything!' For a moment I thought she would actually stamp her foot in vexation. As for the news, I still hadn't digested it—it was still too wriggling and wet to swallow.

'Nobody slept last night, Paul. In. The. Whole. Fucking. World. No one! Well, no. Sarah said she heard on the radio that some people say they slept. Maybe one in a thousand. The radio said the grid crashed in California for four hours because of everyone keeping their lights and TVs on all night. Everybody's totally freaking out about it. Didn't you hear *anything*? I feel like I'm going insane, having to tell you all this!'

She fell onto the couch beside me and began texting with one hand while throwing her other arm over my shoulder, not especially affectionately, but more as a part of the general sprawl of her moment.

'So fucking weird. So *fucking* creepy.'

I tried to make sense of what she'd just said as her fingers henpecked my T-shirt and her phone shuddered. Then she pivoted her head and looked directly at me for the first time since she'd arrived home, her eyes, faintly red-rimmed, locking onto mine.

'Paul. Did you sleep last night?'

I should tell you about my dream now.

In it, I'm walking along the University of British Columbia's West Mall, near the clock tower outside Main Library. On the mall itself stand two ten-foot high cones constructed from long, tapered sheets of mirrored glass. As I pass the south cone, I catch the sun's reflected light, strobing from mirror to mirror. And then the cone explodes with a yawn—like the world is ending, not with a bang or a whimper, but an early bedtime. The sheets of glass don't shatter, they disassemble and drift off into a burning blue sky. Then slowly, I turn toward the library. Everything is floating: trees, people, benches, windows, walls. The pavement beneath my feet gives way, and I tumble into space. The clock tower follows suit, its massive black hands wheeling off in different directions.

Then everything fades until all that's left is the sky and me. My body dissolves next and the sky becomes an all-encompassing sphere of golden light. And then, after a while longer, *I* disappear and there's just the light, an awareness of light. I'm seeing it, but not through eyes, or as if my eyes were all pupil, if that makes any sense. And then time disappears and words cease to be and the light lasts forever. I experience eternity, but still somehow wake up in the morning with a hard-on and a gnawing stomach.

I've had variations on that same dream every night since that first one when Tanya tossed and turned beside me, and it's the most joyous thing I've ever experienced [here I pause, pencil in hand, for a full five minutes before continuing]...despite it all.

By way of compensation, perhaps, bad news gives us a license to overeat. *Screw the Friday night sushi*, Tanya and I decided. Instead, we went all the way back to our sunburned suburban

childhoods—to McDonald's, in other words—and got ourselves two nosebags filled with hot grease and salt. The place
was packed: the floor gritty, the air humid with human heat.
No one in the long queue was particularly hungry; we just
wanted to eat something, all our faces fixed on the same goal of
semi-oblivion through satiation. Emergency room bravado and
sombre denial predominated; people studied the menu board
with furrowed brows and gnawed lips.

'What do you want, babe?' Ahead of us, a fat man in an
irony-free tracksuit spoke to his companion, a woman sporting
an identical outfit, her hair pulled back into a severe ponytail.

'A number two. Diet Coke.'

Just go ahead and order the sugary stuff, I wanted to tell her.
I caught Tanya watching me. She winked, and we burst into
guilty giggles.

'What's so funny?' the woman turned and sniffed, suspecting,
correctly, that *she* was.

'Nothing,' Tanya replied, poker-faced. 'Obviously there's
nothing funny.'

The crowd stared daggers.

After McDonald's, we picked up some Ben and Jerry's at
the packed Safeway then went home and watched the news,
gobbling down burgers and fries from our laps while, on a
parallel track, we gorged on information.

The pundits and experts were trout on the dock, flopping
back and forth in iridescent suits, carping up theories as to why

this was happening, the very *dearth* of facts goading them on. But what does a flopping trout know about *why*? A maniacal cavalcade of ideas was spilling out of their mouths: a solar storm had kept us awake all night; magical mystery waves broadcast by cunning terrorists were to blame! Microwave overload!

Tanya watched with blazing eyes and hunched shoulders, nodding occasionally. I put my arm around her shoulders and rubbed her neck. Every time I tried to speak she shushed me.

The television's caffeinated universe kept unfolding. The flesh-draped skulls of the anchormen and women yammered, and their joke shop teeth chattered. And their eyes! You'd have to handle those twitching eyes carefully if you ever found them in the palms of your hot little hands: you'd have to fight the urge to squeeze their jelly till it squished between your fingers. The men and women on TV were *brazen heads*. Of Irish derivation, a brazen head was omniscient and told those who consulted it whatever they needed to know, past, present, or future: 'let there be a brazen head set in the middle of the place...out of which cast flames of fire'. Isn't that television, exactly? In the centre of things, burning away?

'They're panicking,' Tanya whispered.

'Yes, they are.'

'They don't know any more than we do.'

'No.'

Her cheeks were blotchy and red. 'Then why don't they just shut up?'

On and on through the evening, the Brazen Heads parroted possible explanations that you just knew had been made up moments earlier by other similarly panicked mammals pacing around off-screen. There was consensus on only one point: eight billion cases of insomnia were no coincidence. The odds were on the order of googles and googles to one. It might even have been, as the televangelists and their milky ilk were claiming, the righteous wrath of Great God Almighty, although this theory annoyed me more than the others. If there is a God, then why isn't the presence of His hand acknowledged in everything? Why do we only drag God in when something cool happens (and make no mistake, the unspoken consensus that evening was that the whole mess was sci-fi blockbuster cool)? Why don't people talk about God when McDonald's sells another cheeseburger? *Methinks 'tis God's doing, this sweaty pattie! Yon pimpled youth in the paper cap is naught but his instrument!* Some do! Some people watch granny die, writhing in the arms of cancer, and think that's just fine, part of some big plan. They sound like abuse survivors to me. That said, I suppose my God-unease is similar to my squeamishness about birds: the handlessness of God. I suppose that any of those theories might have been right, but even that first evening I sensed that no explanation was headed our way. What was happening was just a fact. And we weren't a species interested in facts, as such. We were more into evading or spinning them.

At any rate, it all came down to Tonight—all the Heads seemed confident about that much. What would happen *tonight* when we all laid our heads down and either said our prayers or didn't?

* * *

Translucent bags emptied and tossed, Tanya and I salved our salt-scraped tongues with ice cream straight from the bucket. As I ate, I imagined melting goop filtering down among mulched burgers and fries, filling the gaps and soothing my moaning gut.

With our stomachs bloated and the television and the Internet going at it so hot and heavy, the living room soon felt crowded.

'Maybe we should go into the kitchen and leave the laptop and the plasma alone,' I said.

'I almost turned on the radio five minutes ago. I'm so stupid.'

She laughed, but only for a moment, then I spoke into the silence that followed.

'It's weird how we can do that.'

'What?'

'Laugh at ourselves.'

'What do you mean?'

I turned off the television and the room was instantly too silent.

'It's like each of us are two people, one watching the other.'

She thought for a moment. 'I think I get it. Our world,' she threw an arm toward the black screen, which stood there looking for all the world like the Monolith from *2001: A Space Odyssey* tipped over on its side, 'is getting fucked over, but we're also watching it getting fucked over.'

I nodded. 'So there's us getting fucked over and there's also us watching ourselves getting fucked over.'

'Christ, no wonder I can't sleep. But is the part of me that's watching myself get fucked over *also* getting fucked over, Paul?'

It was a good question, I think now. Maybe a great one.

As awareness swelled, tumour-like, in the global consciousness, Tanya's Tinkerbell of a cell phone chimed and shimmied, impelled by all the usual suspects: our parents back in Toronto, her friends and workmates. My mom cried the whole time we spoke while my dad affected a casual dismissiveness about the whole thing that he clearly didn't feel. They weren't different from their normal selves, but neither were they the same. It was as though the volume of their usual personalities had been turned up so high that they were hissing and crackling like a cheap radio at top volume. Indeed, everyone we spoke to that night was nervous and jokey, but circumstance made humour seem like a sinister thing—a guttering cackle etching air in the absence of sense.

At the end of each conversation we said our goodbyes as lightly as we could, but the silences around those words were formal—airless and still.

And yet.

And yet, at the same time, the whole thing was also kind of exciting. Don't be coy; you know what I mean. Tiny disasters—lost kittens, sobbing moppets—could rend our hearts, but the massive ones inevitably became popcorn-munching spectacles.

Viva, some part of our brain always cries, *calamity*. Which may be at least partly why calamity always seemed to find us.

And here's the worst part. Listening to Tanya's conversations as she told friends and relatives about my sleeping, I actually felt myself puffing up a little. How pathetic was that? It turned out that no-one else we knew had slept. I was tempted to feel as though I'd done something *special* by dozing off. It's shameful how we feed on our own scraps of press: the survivor of the mass shooting, the lottery winner, the reality show contestant, the writer of wildly unpopular books on words.

It was almost midnight when we went and looked out the window to see what we feared to see: the blood in our world's stool. All the city's lights were blazing.

We stood there holding hands, feeling each other's poignant skeletons through layers of skin and fat, a nexus of warmth building up between our fingers and palms. We really *were* creatures of pure energy, I remember thinking, just like the hippies and the physicists had always claimed—beings made up of 'energy' and 'wave lengths' and 'vibes', so ephemeral that the swishing of a dryer sheet might neutralize our charges and erase us. Feeling so temporary and fragile was nice; the moment felt valuable.

Tanya squeezed my hand then let go. 'I'd better try to go to sleep. I'm nervous.'

'Let's both go to bed.'

We headed off to the erstwhile big top of our bedroom, took off everything, and pressed our bodies together between the sheets, gerbils in a pet store cage trying to douse our minds and vanish beneath the gaze of incomprehensible giants.

'You sleepy?' I asked as the sheets warmed around us.

Her voice was tiny. 'No. Are you?'

Compassion is—pretty often—omission. I pulled her close, placing my hand over one of her ears, and pressing the other into my chest. And then I yawned.

I think now that if all eight billion of us had just shut off the lights and gone to bed that night and left it alone we'd have all slept and the chalice would have passed us by. But let's be real. Whoever leaves *anything* alone? Life's a scab, and it's our nature to pick at it until it bleeds.

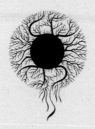

DAY 2
JOHN A' DREAMS

A begging imposter, naked vagabond.

When I woke the next morning it was full daylight and Tanya's side of the bed was a mortuary slab of absence. I found her in the living room. Where the previous morning she'd looked pregnant with unwanted knowledge, she now looked as though she'd given birth, misplaced the baby, and been up all night trying frantically to remember where she'd left it. Was it in the fridge? The laundry hamper? The microwave?

The laptop was open on her blushing bare knees; her eyes were Google goggles.

'How long have you been up?' I asked. Then, 'I'm sorry.'

'No. It's good that one of us could sleep.'

'Nothing?' Nothing. 'Listen, you're just freaked out. You'll sleep when you're tired enough. Everybody will. It's just a...'

Tanya stared down at her laptop, thighs quaking. She pressed down on them, but her hands just started shaking too.

'Do you know how long I have left, Paul? If I don't sleep?'

'I don't want to go in that dir—'

'Thirty two days. Or less. That's what they're saying. Five more days until something called 'sleep deprivation psychosis' sets in. Until I go *insane*, Paul.'

'That's ridiculous. Lots of people have insomnia and they don't go crazy.'

'No. They say even insomniacs doze a little, but this is different. For the last two nights I've been completely awake, all night long. I don't even feel sleepy. So six days to insanity, then thirty two days, max, until total body breakdown and death. Watch. This guy's been on like every five minutes.'

She stabbed the remote at the Monolith, upping the volume. Some lab rat gussied up in a white coat. Bulging eyes, thick eyebrows, and fat lips. I couldn't stand to see the self-importance in his eyes.

'He says they've done studies where they've tried to see how long they can keep people awake, but nobody's ever been able to handle more than six days totally awake before their brains shut down. He thinks that—'

'Turn it off.'

'But I'm not—'

I grabbed the remote, cutting off both Tanya and the rat.

'Let's go out and get some breakfast.'

She didn't say a word as we dressed. I grabbed a printout of my latest draft of *Nod,* and we headed for the nameless greasy spoon where we ate breakfast once a month or so. Eggs, hash browns, toast, and unlimited coffee, all for five dollars a head. Battery eggs, white bread, waxy cheese: the place was a hate crime against both nature and nutrition. The food *tasted* terrible, too—'food in only the strictest technical sense of the word' was how Tanya put it—but the soup kitchen pricing kept us coming back, balanced out the expense of our Friday night sushi fest.

It was a joke between us how we could never remember what the place was called. In fact, it had become our custom to lower our eyes when we approached the restaurant's faded green awning; we didn't want to spoil the fun. The Saturday Breakfast was also a chance for me to run my latest pages past Tanya. And even though this clearly wasn't a normal Saturday morning, it seemed necessary to pretend that it was.

The streets were quiet. Not quiet as in empty, but quiet as in *lots of people, but nobody saying much*. Bright and blustery, then, as we glided down Denman Street among the human beings, none of us fooling anyone with our poorly-performed pantomimes of normalcy. During the early days of colonization, native people, on the verge of starvation and comically outgunned by European religious maniacs, would sometimes profess religious conversion in order to obtain food staples for themselves and their children. In return, our ancestors mocked their desperation by calling them Rice Christians. Well, that morning in Vancouver we were all Rice Christians, treading lightly, hoping not to piss God off. Which was a good thing because all around us was a city of glass.

Green glass apartment towers in the background of every breeze-blown view, big glass fronts on all the stores—the West End was a place where everybody wanted to see and be seen: a place for promenading, for reflections and transparency. All that glass added up to a kind of war cry: *this is how mighty we are, this is how bold: we'll build a city out of glass on the edge of the ocean, God, and dare you to smash it down*. No fear of insurrection or weather, of hurricanes or invasion, the towers declared in their gargantuan fragility. The wind was a mere amusement, a pretend-wind threading its way between the skyscrapers like a clown with a handful of balloons weaving through a birthday party. And in the face of all this smiling glass, the people walking by had seemed indestructible, as dense and centred as black holes. Until this morning. Now the city had tipped somehow and we were all slowly sliding toward English Bay.

Strangeness glazed all the normal sights; everything looked the same as before, but no one could have taken in the scene and not known something was very different. This morning we were a city of glassy eyes.

'Those guys,' Tanya whispered, pointing to a gay couple and their matching black labs, 'They aren't walking their dogs. Their dogs are walking them.'

And I saw it, literally saw her metaphor made real. The dogs looked calm and confident while the humans attached to the other end of their leashes were mere dragged baggage.

What else? I looked around.

All eyes were directed inward; everyone had their introspecs on. As we passed silent bakeries and cafes we could see money changing hands; we could hear the clink of coins being counted then splatting onto marble counters. People hunched across tables, reading one another's lips.

'As if what they're whispering about isn't exactly what everyone else is whispering about,' Tanya said loudly, causing a few heads to turn, first toward us—then quickly away.

Reaching the restaurant, we sat down at a table by the open front window and ordered from the waitress. She was a tank-faced woman of Slavic descent who looked like she'd spent her youth being fed steroids in some old Soviet bloc waitress training facility. Then we settled into silence, scrutinizing our cutlery. Some mornings there'd be dried egg yolk on the tines of one of our forks, and we'd call the waitress over. She'd replace the utensil without apology, indeed, with something verging on contempt for our bourgeois, our *kulak* squeamishness.

I turned my knife in the sun, and as it flashed I remembered my dream. Two nights in a row. I was just going to tell Tanya about it when I saw, heading straight toward us, Charles.

How to introduce Charles into this narrative?

While my lack of enthusiasm kept the bulk of humanity at arm's length, it almost seemed to attract people like Charles. Maybe it's the fact that we misanthropes don't discriminate—the people hater hates everybody equally. Maybe this sad sack egalitarianism makes the Charleses of the world, used as they are to being dismissed out of hand, feel raised to uncommon heights of social desirability when bathed in its jaundiced glow.

Charles smelled bad. What more do I really need to say? He

was an outsider always looking for a way in. But no one would let him in. Instead, we relegated him to the status of dumpster diving 'local character'. As though he were fictional.

I can say of myself that I have no time for people until I understand them, and then I whiplash all the way from contempt to pity. A shitty way to live: the worst of everything. Contempt is bad, but pity's worse. Pity's sticky: it clings to the poor fool who presumes to be in a safe enough place from whence to do the commiserating.

'Oh shit.' Tanya had seen him.

'Hey, Paul.' Charles spoke to me but looked down at the empty chair beside her.

'Hi Charles.'

I'd never learned his last name; we'd never been introduced. I only knew his *first* name because people spoke about him behind his back when he left the table. Always Charles. Never Chuck, never Charlie. The formality a shuffling away.

'How's the new book coming, Paul?'

Involuntarily, I glanced down at my manuscript on the chair beside me and prayed he wouldn't notice it. Charles knew I wrote. Had checked my books out from the Joe Fortes library where he and dozens of other floaters spent their days. Checked them out and, oddly enough, read them.

'Slow.' He probably thought the whole world spoke in Tarzan-like monosyllables. But you couldn't shut him down with curt replies—brevity just opened up more space for *his* words.

'Okay if I sit?' he asked, preemptively folding himself into an empty chair.

Charles had the red plastic face of someone who lived rough. His expression was friendly, but fixed that way, as though with bobby pins or staples. He was fairly tall but came across short, with all the awkwardness and crumpledness that entails—like a hinged skeleton you pull out of a cardboard box each Halloween and half-heartedly thumbtack to your front door.

'How's Miss Soviet Union 1962 this morning?'

As he said this, Charles glanced around to make sure the waitress wasn't near. He was invoking a triangle of intimacy: *we* three were talking about *her*. She was the outsider, not him.

'She's okay.'

'You're too nice. I bet she's not going to sell much coffee this morning.'

'It's not funny, Charles,' Tanya said, as though to a floor-peeing puppy.

'Starbucks is going to be empty today. And I quote, *"The New York Times* reports that the American Starbucks chain has been forced to shut down a thousand outlets in the last year." And that was before. People are no longer buying into—. It's definitely a broadcast from the new Russian-Chinese satellite string, Paul. It's like something out of an Ian Fleming novel.' He pronounced it 'Fleeming'. 'They're disrupting our brainwaves with some sort of static. We'll start to panic and the markets will fall apart, just like after 911, then after a couple of days they'll march in and buy us all up. It's so obvious.'

'Yeah, but the Chinese aren't sleeping either. So where does that leave you?'

The waitress slapped our plates down on the table.

'No. No satellite. God.'

We all stared as sunlight made brutal cement of her skin.

'And *why* would God do this to us?' Charles said finally, supercilious for my benefit.

'Because of faggots and terrorists and the shit television, stupid street bum. God is telling us no rest for the wicked. Now He will see who listens to Him.'

She folded tuberous arms across her chest. There was no room for the conditional or hypothetical in the woman's English; she was all declaratives and imperatives.

It was too much for Tanya, who had no time for Bible babblers, having been raised by a couple and having moved across a continent to escape their take on bliss.

'You keep your hateful opinions to yourself, or I'll talk to the owner.'

There was spittle on Tanya's lower lip, and she wiped it away without self-consciousness.

The waitress smirked.

'Fuck you,' she said, then turned and left us.

'Fuck you too, *bitch*!' Tanya screamed after her, a single vein throbbing blue in the centre of her forehead.

'Can you believe that?' Charles asked me eagerly. 'What do you think about all this, Paul? You look pretty well-rested. Did you sl—?'

'And fuck you too, *Charles*.' Tanya whirled back around.

'I don't—'

'Nobody asked you to join us. Nobody ever asks you to join them. Ever shut up long enough to wonder why?'

Charles jumped up, hiding his hands behind his back, like he'd been bad.

'I didn't mean to intrude,' he said, his face growing redder.

Tanya laughed, possessed by the cruel ghost of two nights' lost sleep.

'Intrude. *Please*. Disturbing people is all you ever do. Don't insult us by pretending you don't know that.'

'Tanya...' I began.

'*Tanya*,' she mimicked. 'Am I wrong? *Is* he welcome? Did you want him to come over? Shall we order him the Special?'

Charles backed across the room, his eyes fixed on mine, bumping into chair after chair until he disappeared out a back door that led into the alley. We sat silently, Tanya staring at her congealing food and me at mine. The egg yolks were lemon meringue where they should have been tangerine. A vision of caged, armless mothers flashed through my mind, but I shook it off.

'Did you have to do that?'

'He was going to ask you if you were a Sleeper.'

And that was the first time I heard the word used in its new sense—capitalized. Had Tanya picked it up off the television or had she coined it herself? Or were a few billion frazzled brains simultaneously beginning to name this new reality?

'So?'

'I just didn't think it was a good idea to tell him.'

'Why not?'

'I don't know why not, Paul. No reason I guess. But fuck him anyway. I don't have time for it. Let's just eat.'

We did our best with the food we'd been given but only managed crusts and coffee. After a while, one of us, I can't remember who, said, 'This is only the beginning, isn't it?'

We both looked around then and the restaurant was empty, no waitress, no Charles, no other customers. Just like no one had set foot in the place for a thousand years.

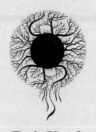

DAY 3
NAILS DRIVEN INTO
COTTAGE WALLS

*This was a Roman practice under the notion
that it kept off the plague.*

At 8am the next morning something called the International
Microwave Communication Ban went into effect. Someone in
an office somewhere took a deep breath, exhaled and flipped
a switch. Instantly, ISPs and cell service providers around
the world went down. More switches were flipped and the
landlines went silent too. The night before, posters had gone up
all over the city announcing that Xbox controllers and garage
door openers were now verboten. The idea was to bring down
the walls of static that permeated our lives and see if we could
unclench our brains and snooze in the resulting stillness.

Then, at 8:01, it hit me. Tanya and I were on our own. The

network of threads binding us to family and friends had been torn down. Suddenly distance became real, probably for the first time in our lives. Toronto was infinitely distant and even the condos of friends across English Bay seemed impossibly far away.

Was it time to mourn yet? Almost, almost.

Although the ban was UN-sanctioned and backed by the threat of military force, there were rumours that Russia and China weren't playing fair, that they were keeping an electronic exoskeleton of services online in order to avoid what would have to be devastating impacts on their economic, military, and political infrastructures. No doubt they were—and no doubt we were too.

At 9am uniforms appeared. The police, the army, the fire brigade, and for all I knew, the SPCA—the powers-that-be deployed anyone who could lay their hands on some sort of official-looking outfit into the streets. Vans with antennae cruised past slow and coy, followed by jeeps loaded down with gum-chewing reservists. Why did good-hearted Canadian boys, brought up with the sweet succor of liberal marijuana laws and universal health care, suddenly look so badass and American the moment you slapped a uniform on their backs and handed them a pack of Juicy Fruit?

I was out there in the thick of it, trying to get to the Safeway to stock up on provisions. There was a lineup of around five hundred people outside of the store. People were being admitted in groups of ten by a group of soldiers at the door. 'Cash only' read a handwritten sign, inevitable now that credit and debit cards were defunct. And how long until the centuries-long spell was broken, money turned back into paper, and we reverted to bartering eyes for eyes and teeth for teeth?

'Any idea how long it takes to get in?' I asked the woman ahead of me.

She didn't reply but simply shook her head stiffly and shuffled forward.

The answer was it took three hours.

When I finally reached the door, my entry was blocked by a pock-marked soldier with a twitch in his eyes that made me think he was winking ironically each time he spoke.

'Arms up.'

'Sure.'

He patted me down, pulled my cell phone out of my jacket pocket, and tossed it into a pile of electronic devices behind him. A half million dollars' worth of high tech goodies reduced to the status of broken old Transformers toys.

'Why are you taking them? They don't work anyway.'

'Got cash?'

'Yes.'

'How much?'

'Fifty or sixty bucks.'

He snorted. 'That should get you a pack of bologna. Happy shopping.'

He stood aside, and I went in.

I soon saw what he meant. All the nicely-printed shelf tags had been pulled off and prices written directly on the goods in red felt pen. They were now roughly triple what they'd been two days ago. At least capitalism was still alive and functioning properly. The thought of that invisible hand still busily bitch-slapping the poor and desperate was almost reassuring. After all, in order to muster up the will to profiteer, one needs to be able to envision a future in which to spend one's ill-gotten gains.

The shelves were rapidly emptying. I checked my wallet and thought fast. My three twenty dollar bills weren't going to go far, so I had to think protein. More than that, I had to think *unpopular* protein. In the peanut butter section, a T-shirt-shredding fist fight had broken out between two burly men. A shattered glass jar lay on the floor between them as they wrestled above the slimy, jagged mess.

In the ethnic aisle I got lucky and caught sight of a half dozen jars of tahini at the back of a top shelf. Survival of the tallest. I grabbed four—all I could afford. Then, clutching the jars to my chest, I pushed my way toward the checkout stand.

Coming out of the store I saw that the line had now swelled to a couple of thousand panicky people who were surging forward against the line of soldiers. Something ugly was going to happen soon. An idea had to be growing in that massive line up: *why pay when every defenseless person leaving the store with an armful of groceries is a sort of walking Food Bank?*

Not liking my chances of making it safely through the parking lot with my meagre purchases, I took a hard right and headed around the side of the building, stuffing the jars of tahini into my jacket and zipping it up tight.

The loading zone behind the building was deserted except for a dreadlocked young woman and her kindergarten-aged daughter who sat on a low kerb. The mother looked to be the sort of ersatz hippie whose long skirt and high-maintenance hair were about all that separated her from a typical welfare mom. She was crying openly, while her daughter stared at me, unfazed.

'What's wrong?' I asked, fatally.

'Three guys. They took our food and ran off that way.' She pointed toward the parking lot, screamed 'Fucking bastards!!' then covered her face and sobbed some more. Was her story true? Did it matter?

'Here.' I unzipped my jacket and took out a jar, giving it to the little girl. That old devil pity. 'Do you live far from here?'

'Two blocks.' She answered cautiously, seemingly afraid that I was about to appoint myself their protector and house guest.

'Then get going and lock the doors behind you when you get there.'

She still looked suspicious. 'Okay. Thanks.'

They got up to leave, but I stopped them, took out another jar and handed it to the little girl. She smiled up at me but said nothing.

'Is your daughter okay?' I asked.

'She hasn't said a word in two days. But she still—'

Deciding against sharing the obvious fact that her daughter still slept, the woman grabbed the child's hand, and they turned and ran.

* * *

Walking home was like visiting a rapidly-degenerating patient in intensive care. Commerce was almost done; the chain stores were down for the count but some mom and pop places were still open, but warily, looking at the sidewalks through slitted windows, though they had little left to sell except for magazines and car air fresheners.

Menace was in the air. I didn't see anything YouTube-worthy, but the indefinable strangeness I'd noticed when Tanya and I went out for breakfast the day before had grown a little less indefinable overnight. People's faces were the big indicators of what was going on. People's faces looked like shit. Men weren't shaving and women weren't doing their hair. Everything and everyone was starting to look slightly greasy. Slightly off-one's-meds and teetering-on-the-edge-of-one's-rocker. And cops. There were cops and soldiers everywhere. They clutched guns and stood in clusters on the corners, waiting, blue and green. Shattered cell phones like smashed candy on the pavement.

That night Tanya started begging me for sex.

I hope that doesn't sound even slightly erotic because I do mean *begging*. She'd become obsessed by the idea that if I could only fuck her into insensibility, she'd break through whatever wall of static surrounded her and sleep. And she had support in this belief: in the twenty-first century there was always plenty of support for any old thing you might care to have a crack at believing. The previous day she'd been glued to the television, watching, transfixed, as people called into talk shows and claimed in loud voices that they'd made themselves sleep through any number of methods, sex marathons being fourth on the list, right after drinking, praying, and drugging. What was fifth? I can't remember. Maybe shopping. The sleep-claimers were all crackpots, needless to say, but it didn't matter: crackpotism was going mainstream. I imagined the next issue of *Cosmopolitan*, if it ever came out: *50 Hot New Ways to Screw Yourself into Dreamland!*

'Paul. Fuck me.'

Without waiting for a reply, she marched into the bedroom and stripped. I hesitated in the doorway as she knelt on the mattress, hands clasped before her, forehead resting on her knuckles, offering up her pale ass. She looked like a pantomime horse: her rear half ready for fornication, her front seemingly engaged in prayer. Confronted by the odd couple of her dishevelled vagina and sternly puckered asshole, I bit my lower lip and looked away. Nobody wants sex to be too naked. Not completely naked. It was a terrible moment, almost awful enough to wipe away other, better memories of our lovemaking.

'Come *on!*'

I can still hear the contempt in her voice. At times everyone wonders how deeply buried contempt is beneath the surface of their friends' and lovers' smiles; most of us suspect—accurately, I believe—that it lies in a shallow grave, gasping for breath beneath a damp mulch of manners and restraint. Was there ever such a thing as unconditional love? It's hard to say, given that those closest to us always seemed to want or need the most. The purest love we ever had was probably for strangers or imaginary people: for Mother Theresa or Santa Claus. Or babies, before they got branded or tattooed with identity, or old people after theirs had been spayed and neutered by dementia or waning libido.

I have a theory. By now this won't surprise you. My theory is that we needed love because we were so hard to like. Simple, huh? We're so unworthy of anything, so wavering, so temporary. All love was pain in that it was rooted in pity for our wretched souls. And yet, only love could hope to hold us together. And without love?

'Come *on*.'

Contempt pooling. Deepening. *It isn't her*, I told myself. *It's just what's happening to her.* To us.

'Tanya, I can't just—'

'Remember that afternoon at the Pan Pacific last summer?' she asked, twisting around to scowl at me over one freckled shoulder.

The Pan Pacific was a luxury hotel beloved of rich Asian tourists and lumpy old we-earned-it-so-now-we-better-spend-it Canadians in town for some high-end shopping. It was only five blocks from our apartment, but once in a while we treated ourselves to a night there, considering the erotic jumpstart of an unfamiliar bed well worth the expense. Those elegant rooms must have been invisibly splattered with decades and gallons of cum and sweat, no doubt, and vomit and shit and tears. But you couldn't see any of that and the room was always new to us when we knelt on the bed, facing one another.

There in the now, Tanya rolled onto her back and crossed her ankles.

'Remember how I pretended I was a desperate actress who thought she was auditioning for a commercial, and you were the sneaky porn guy holding auditions?' Now she was using her seductive voice, and it was creeping me out. 'I did that for you, Paul, even though I thought it was borderline fucked-up. So do this for me now.'

And so I tried.

I could barely get an erection, only managing after a few minutes of near-frantic pumping, courtesy of Tanya's white-knuckled right hand. She got back onto all fours. The odd couple again: a beige fleck of shit in the crinkles of her asshole; a rawness to the lips of her vagina.

She came after five minutes or so, a pinched half-orgasm that wasn't going to do the trick, wasn't even going to raise her hopes.

'Don't stop.'

I didn't. There was no way I was going to come myself, which was lucky. I kept at it for as long as I could stand, maybe forty minutes or so, until my knees burned and my erection diminished, first transforming into a half-filled water balloon, then into nothing much at all. Eventually, I flopped out and lay beside her, rubbing my knees. She stared at the ceiling while I stared at her profile. At the three day mark, Tanya actually looked better than she had after two days, like her old self but in slightly sharper focus.

I blinked back tears. We were going to grow old together, either in a couple of decades or a couple of weeks and maybe there wasn't as much difference between those two timelines as I'd have thought forty-eight hours earlier. And if Tanya only had four weeks left, the same lessons would need to be learned, the same pride swallowed, as if we had incontinence and dementia to look forward to.

But we probably didn't.

As the blood flowed back into my calves, Tanya's rib cage rose and fell.

'The transmission ban—'

'It won't change anything.'

'You don't know that.'

She turned her head my way.

'You don't know that, either.'

'Well, and you don't know *that*.'

'And so on.'

Tanya moved toward me and nestled her face under my chin. Horribly enough, I felt my penis begin to stir again. The incipient erection felt stupid and slug-like against my thigh. I shifted slightly, hoping to conceal it from her.

'I think it's time we started planning for what comes next.'

'Why don't we just go to sleep?'

'I'm not *going* to sleep, Paul.'

I heard myself begin to whine.

'You don't know that. That's just something out of a movie. Doomed people in movies always have this sad foreknowledge of what's coming down the pike. But that's just Hollywood bullshit melodrama. You don't *know* you're not going to sleep.'

She struggled to keep her temper as she composed a response to my idiot optimism.

'We have to start planning for what's going to happen next.

Even if you're right and it doesn't last, we still have to plan. If I'm wrong, we'll laugh about it in a couple of days.'

I swallowed, twin feelings tugging at my trachea. A passionate desire to save the woman I loved. And something else—a bastard thought I couldn't control: *If it's going to happen, it's going to happen.* An idea as inevitable as math.

Everybody dies eventually. So if eight billion of us die in the next four weeks is that *significant?* All this sleeplessness plague could do was align those billions of inevitable deaths into a slightly narrower window of time—a matter of efficiency, not tragedy. If, during any one of a million previous nights, a giant asteroid had smashed the earth into gravel while we all slept, would it have *mattered?* With no one left to mourn the wreckage, one could even argue that it wouldn't be a bad way to end things at all: egalitarian if nothing else. I even thought of a scene in *Star Wars* where Princess Leia receives news that her home world has been destroyed by Darth Vader's Death Star. She throws a hairy fit, but two scenes later, she's back to flirting with Han Solo.

I slapped these thoughts down, hating myself.

'Listen, Tanya. There's no way this will keep on. First thing is we're going to get you out of the city. We'll head north, find a—'

A knock on the apartment door. Having forgotten there was a world outside, I started, then got up and threw on my old grey dressing gown.

'Look first, Paul. Don't just open up the door. Anybody could be out there.'

I went and squinted through the peephole, wondering if

a crazed mob would be outside, if a crazed mob would even fit in our narrow hall. But all I saw was the old woman who lived next door. Mrs Simmons. A widow but still married to the corpse who'd bullied the bulk of her life away. Old man Simmons had been, she'd confided to Tanya more than once in the elevator's confessional, a real piece of shit—his communion with the world a binary code made up of rapidly alternating slaps and silences.

In the fishbowl of the peephole, Mrs Simmons' faded face darted left and right. She was a skinny old thing but with jowls that gave her the appearance of having a puppet's hinged jaw; when she spoke, someone else seemed to be pulling the strings.

When I opened the door, she jumped back and pressed against the opposite wall, cowering in her pink tracksuit. Three nights without sleep had left the old woman sucked juice-box dry.

'Are you okay, Mrs Simmons?'

She became aggressive with her bony chin. 'That noise. Is that noise coming out of your place?'

'What noise?' For a moment I thought the poor woman had overheard our sex efforts, but then I remembered that our bedroom was on the wrong side of the apartment for that to be the case. That and how silent our fucking had been.

Mrs Simmons peeled herself off the wall and inched toward me, glaring.

'Don't tell me you don't hear it!'

It's always bad news when the meek get assertive: an order, a question, a threat, and a plea all rolled into one. In Heaven, the Bible and Bono both say, all the colours bleed into one; in Hell, I've since learned, feelings do the same thing. Swampwater was what we called the various Slurpee flavours we mixed into one cup as kids, one on top of the other. Neon pink, lime green, cola brown. Another hole in the language, another new word of my own invention. The old woman's voice swampwatered with feelings.

'If I don't tell you that, Mrs Simmons, then I don't know what else I *can* tell you.'

'You,' her words rattled in her throat. 'You. You hear it. Don't lie to me. It's coming from the walls, or maybe from outside.' Then she tried on a little girl voice. 'Please don't lie. It's unkind.'

Suddenly, Tanya was behind me.

'We haven't heard anything, Mrs Simmons. Promise. It's probably just nerves. Everyone is—'

The old lady's tongue flicked at the cracked corners of her mouth. 'Don't tell me about nerves. I know about nerves. I know nerves from forty years back. I knew nerves back before nerves were even invented. Someone's out there humming slow and low. It's quiet, but you can hear it if you listen.'

'I don't hear anything, I swear.'

Her expression broke apart. 'Don't lie! Oh, God, there's no reason! If we lie to each other there'll be no one to turn to. And if there's no one to turn to then—'

'But we don't hear—'

Mrs Simmons snapped her head around and fixed us with hateful eyes, suddenly another someone else.

'I said no lies!' Then she changed again and her voice took on a childish inflection once more. 'It's a terrible thing to do to an old woman! Please think about what you're doing, Paul.'

It was as though she was thrashing back and forth in time, from pleading, uncomprehending child to bitter, denying adult.

She swooped down to a whisper. 'Pretending it's not happening won't make it go away. You can't ignore it.'

I looked at Tanya, wondering for a moment if she heard something like what Mrs Simmons was describing. Catching my glance, she narrowed her eyes and shook her head sharply, furious about whatever it was she saw in my expression.

Then the power went out and in the dull glow of the emergency lights, we looked at one another. None of us expected it to go on again.

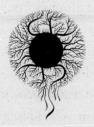

DAY 4
ACCIDENTAL COLOURS

Those which depend on the state of our eye, and not
those which the object really possesses, as when coming
into a dark room from the sun. The accidental colour
of red is bluish-green, of black, white.

'Excuse me?'

Framed by lengthening light, the man in the orange hazard vest stared at nothing. I spoke, but he didn't reply—just stood there as though stillness was mankind's natural state, as though we were a race of Easter Island figures. He was a Stop Sign Guy: a giant red lollipop tight in his right hand, he was one of a group of city workers attempting to repair a power pole that had been knocked down that morning in the alley behind our apartment. A runaway Brinks truck, since duly sacked and towed, had done the deed.

A shock to see them working. *Why fix a power pole when the power is gone?* I suppose the answer was too obvious, too bedrock, for me to see, even then. To my credit, however, I was beginning to understand that incredulity was now an outmoded response to unfolding events.

Tanya frowned and waved her hand in front of his glazed eyes. 'Hey? Anybody in there?'

While the rest of his crew stood huddled beside their crane, talking intensely, Stop Sign Guy's head tilted slightly back as he stared through the blushing sky toward almost-visible stars above and beyond, his mouth agape. In addition to 'hanging open', 'agape' also means love, as in the way our mouths go slack when we see Beauty. It's an ancient Greek word, used in more recent times by Martin Luther King Jr. to describe what he termed 'disinterested love'—Jesus love, Buddha love. Stop Sign Guy had become a slack-jawed statue. Were statues, I wondered, filled with love? Were they enchanted men and women, jaws hanging slack, who'd been flash-frozen by beauty? Had they seen something that had brought their world to a standstill? Were they beings somehow beyond us, beyond our grasping, snapping little world, transfixed by infinity? Agape, just like me—in my dream?

He was a bony little fellow with nicotine fingers. Young but somehow done with youth. I've observed that people whose career trajectories arc toward the holding of stop signs eight hours a day are either really thin or really fat. And they all smoke.

We were about to turn and walk away when, suddenly, Stop Sign Guy was back from wherever he'd been. His mouth closed, he swallowed, and we made eye contact.

He smiled. 'Sorry. What was that?'

Casual, as though nothing strange was going on. The television had said this would happen: momentary space-outs coupled with a band-of-pressure feeling around the skull right around day four or five. Stop Sign Guy smiled helplessly, the kind of fellow who had questionable taste in music and disturbing taste in movies but who would come over on short notice to help you move something heavy. And be truly grateful for the beer he'd receive as payment.

'Our car's parked behind your crane. We were just wondering how long you guys are going to be.'

Tanya and I had come up with a plan: we were going to drive out of the city before things got really ugly, most likely really soon. Some tycoon's empty mansion up at Whistler would suit us well, we thought. Might as well find somewhere nice for the little woman to lose her mind and for me to stretch out my arms and greet the apocalypse. Or maybe it was simpler than a plan: maybe we were just getting incredibly motivated to take flight.

The night before had been loud, even louder than the preceding day. Looking out our windows we'd been able to see that while the rot hadn't spread noticeably further on the surface of things, it had dug deeper and plunged its roots into the city's bloodstream. People running around like spiders, darting in and out of shadows beneath the full moon, intentions unfathomable. Picture an old apple whose skin hasn't yet collapsed—but beneath that skin the flesh is soft as cheesecake. You sense, smell even, that it's gone rotten, but you don't know for sure until you touch it and feel it yield beneath the slightest pressure of your thumb.

We heard the occasional gunshot, but easily adapted to that: if anything, given the hard lessons TV news and cop shows had taught us all our lives, it seemed odd that sporadic gunfire *hadn't* been a normal part of life all along.

Stop Sign Guy was gone again. Hard hat off, he was massaging the back of his head, like his memory was knotted up back there. Bundles of nerves roping up from his body into his brain. Yank them, I couldn't stop myself from thinking, and he'd jerk.

'Hey! Asshole! What's your problem?!'

A man in tan overalls, a rage of muscles knotted beneath his superhero-tight T-shirt, had broken off from the group by the crane and was striding toward us. A creature of the gym, he was all swollen limbs and chest. As he neared us, I thought of Blemmyes, headless mythical creatures, their eyes, nose, and mouth lodged in their chests.

'It's no biggie, Al.' Stop Sign Guy was back and speaking up in my defence.

The Blemmye ignored his crew mate and snarled at me through gritted teeth. 'I said, 'What's your *problem?*' asshole.'

There was a question behind his question, and that shadow question was 'Do you want to dance?'

The Blemmye moved toward me, and I took a step backward: the opening figure in our mambo.

'I was just asking when you guys were going to be finished. Our car—'

Then I was on the ground, and he was on top of me, swinging drum-taut fists into my sides. The back of my head felt damp and warm; I'd either landed in a puddle of hot soup or I was bleeding. My arms went up to protect my face, but when I realized my ribs were about to be broken I forced them down, lying at attention while he pummelled my biceps and elbows.

And then I found I didn't much mind.

I felt the pain, or rather saw pain fireworks exploding before my eyes. Physical pain was suddenly just nerve information, a series of tiny electrical charges whose combined voltage wouldn't be sufficient to power up a small mouse's iPod. I was curiously detached.

And so instead of screaming for help or begging for mercy, I simply lay there and watched the Blemmye's face as it swung at me again and again, now panting with exertion. A shrieking demon. Or a wailing baby. Or a professional wrestler, mid-orgasm, perhaps. And what was that streaming in his eyes? Rage? Fear? Shock? Sadness? All of them? Slowly, my field of vision saturated with strange cellophane colours. I saw the faces of Stop Sign Guy and the other crew members behind the Blemmye's hulking shoulders as he leaned into his work. Their bared teeth were animal signals for their own swampwatering emotions: the same Trick or Treat Mrs Simmons had been offering the night before.

Time took a hike then, the Blemmye's blows registering like silent exclamation points, until interrupted by a shrill scream that had to be coming from Tanya—a distant, soaring cry horrified to find itself naked in the open air.

'You're killing him!'

The beating didn't last long after that. Violence stale-dates; you can't just pound away at a man until all that's left is a red puddle seeping into the ground; you can't take someone much past hamburger, really, not even if you're a serial killer or Gitmo interrogator. Soon enough, hands appeared on the Blemmye's torso and dragged it off me. Three generic cops who'd appeared out of nowhere.

'You shouldn't have pushed him,' the Blemmye howled, straining against an octopus of arms. The creature's humanity was, as far as I could see, gone. Did it even have a head? I didn't think so. I'm still not sure.

'Pushed him? I never—'

'Ray, he didn't push me,' Stop Sign Guy said, eyes flicking back and forth between the creature and me. 'Why're you saying that, dude?'

The Blemmye howled and increased its struggles.

'If you can walk, you better get out of here, man,' one of the cops told me. He jerked his chin toward Stop Sign Guy. 'You too, pal.'

'Why are you mad at *me*?' Stop Sign Guy whined, backing down the alley. 'What did I do? It's not fair.'

Listening to Stop Sign Guy's voice, I felt like getting up and pummelling him myself. *Not fair.* Words like 'fair' or 'reason' seemed aligned with antiquated concepts like 'vapours' or 'humours' or 'ether'. Similarly, 'why' seemed a completely ludicrous path of enquiry. *Why are you beating me, sirrah?* On Birchin Lane it's the last question that needs asking; on Birchin Lane it's a pathetic question, an admission of weakness and defeat. To use the old jailhouse term and not the modern rock and roll one, a *punk's* question.

As if to prove my thesis, the Blemmye now turned toward Stop Sign Guy and began to gnash and strain in his departing direction, tendons popping.

Tanya helped me to my feet, and I steadied myself against a Smithrite that reeked of puke and putrefaction.

The cops had their guns out now, one pressed to each side of the Blemmye's head. It was like something out of a Tarantino remake of the Three Stooges: if they both shot, they'd kill each other as well as my attacker.

'Shut up, motherfucker! Shut the fuck up!'

'Paul,' Tanya whispered, 'Can you walk?'

I nodded.

'Stand back, give me a shot at him!' one cop cried.

The other cop crabwalked backward while his partner stood up and pointed his gun down toward the Blemmye's heart while speaking softly. 'You stupid motherfucker. You pathetic fucking piece of shit.'

The Blemmye was writhing like a beetle on its back, arms and legs thrashing as it sought to avoid the gun's glare.

We staggered down the alley and onto Denman Street. No one followed us. Seconds later we heard a shot and a loud whoop but kept moving.

A lot of broken glass on the sidewalk: trip and you'd cut yourself badly. Yesterday there had been big shards but today the glass had been crunched down into slivers. Tomorrow, perhaps, it would be a crystal powder: Vancouver distilled to its snortable essence.

Our footsteps as we minced along sounded like boots trudging through crusted snow. There were people everywhere, leaning against doorways, sitting on benches and staring, acres of space around them all, all of them looking like leftovers pushed to the back of the fridge.

Two police cars moved slowly down the street as we turned onto Davie, heading east. All the other vehicles, many of them with their windshields smashed and their roofs caved in, were parked or abandoned in the middle of the road.

'Does it hurt?'

'Yeah.'

'Those fucking *maniacs*.' She screamed the last word over her shoulder then turned back to me. 'Listen, we've got to get you to St. Paul's. That's at least fifteen blocks away. Do you think you can walk that far? I don't think we'll be able to—there aren't any cabs.'

Her voice was pulling me back from wherever I'd been.

'I'll try.'

Dusk, the Blindman's Holiday. Too dark to work by daylight and too soon to light candles. A rheumy-eyed mutt stood in the middle of the sidewalk watching us. He didn't move, so we stepped around him. Dogs behave differently at night than they do during the day. Not just now: it's always been that way. At night the ones that have a bone to pick with humankind come growling a little nearer than they would in full sunlight while the frightened, shrinking ones slink a little deeper into the shadows. Now the same thing was happening to the people.

With the deepening of evening, some of the shadowy figures we encountered looked away when I glanced in their direction while others stared back hard, their pupils black and sharp. A week ago I would have thought they were playing tough, but now I saw that it was more than that. They were trying to make us into objects, to force our eyes down and strip away our humanity. Look down and lose or stare back and be prepared for a fight? The old urban conundrum had taken on a sinister new urgency; choices that, until a few days ago, had only to be made in crack alleys or biker bars were now popping up, like toadstools, all around us.

Tanya stopped. Unprepared, I stumbled against her. She turned and searched my eyes.

'What's with you, Paul?'

'What do you mean?'

'What I mean is you're not showing any emotion. That fucking gym ape back there was going to kill you. You know?'

'I know.'

'And you're not that brave. You should be shaking in your boots.'

She was pushing at buttons, hoping to trigger some outrage, but I didn't have any to offer her.

'I know that too.'

'Well?'

'The beating didn't hurt. And it didn't scare me. I don't know why.'

She rubbed her temples with the tips of her fingers, then spoke through gritted teeth. 'It doesn't make any sense. You're supposed to be taking care of me! What am I doing babysitting you?'

She was right, of course. And *that* hurt, even if the beating hadn't. There were black rings under Tanya's eyes, and her makeup was poorly applied, resulting in a kind of fuzziness around her face that made it hard for me to look at her. It was time to man up and play the strong, silent part. There was no way I could tell her about the Blemmye now. Thinking of the absurdity of the situation I laughed, as much from a dearth of options as from any other cause.

'What's so fucking funny, Paul?' Tanya pushed me away and stepped back in revulsion. 'It's not funny!

I slumped, clenching my stomach muscles to keep myself upright.

'Nothing. Nothing's funny. Just like at McDonald's the other night. Let's just keep moving.'

Down a side street a group of young men were walking in our direction, hooting, but not, so far as I could see, at us. Not yet. Suddenly I was very much aware of Tanya's attractiveness— that and the limp that marked me as easy prey.

I started doing my best to feign a normal stride. On the next block, a tall man in a dirty woollen overcoat, hair long and stringy, leaned against the brick wall of a bank next to a darkened ATM, watching us. He could have been a hobo, could have been a poseur; for years it had been getting harder and harder to tell the difference. When we passed him, he began to follow, stopping when we stopped, walking when we walked.

'What's your problem?' Tanya yelled at one point.

He didn't reply, just stood there, watching us and breathing with his whole body.

After a while we ignored him. Lions and gazelles on the Serengeti. I ask you: what else was there to do?

By the time we were a block from Burrard Street and the hospital, it was dark. We passed through the parking lot of a locked-down Shopper's Drug Mart, its barred windows and doors a set of gritted teeth. I glanced over at Tanya.

A red dot was bobbing on her forehead.

'There's some sort of light shining on your face,' I whispered. 'I think it's a laser sight.'

She wrinkled her brow. 'What are you...?'

'Look.' Grunting, I pulled her to one side and stuck my free hand up in the air to catch the firefly.

For a moment she stared at the red spot wriggling on my palm, still not comprehending. Then, in tandem, we looked up into the forest of blind skyscrapers that surrounded us.

'Where's it coming from?' she whispered.

'I don't know.' I dropped my hand a half a heartbeat before a patch of the asphalt behind us shattered. The red light began to dance crazily on the ground. Another shot. And then another.

Tanya grabbed my hand and dragged me toward the loading dock at the rear of the hospital. A fourth shot, this time right in front of us. Blinded by grit from the flying asphalt we stopped and turned, ants thwarted by a small boy's hand. We made as if to move toward the drug store, but the red dot shook its head while our feet lurched this way and that inside shoes that seemed glued to the ground.

Then the light was gone, and we heard laughter.

At first I thought it was the invisible gunman, but it wasn't him—it was the guy in the trench coat who'd been following us. He was standing in the middle of the parking lot, about thirty feet behind us, dancing with the beam of light. The red spot travelled a ticklish path up and down his torso, then across his face. He'd step and the light would move to him. He laughed and nodded at us and didn't seem so threatening anymore; he looked like he wanted us to be in on the joke.

Then the light fixed on his chest. A fifth shot and he fell, breakdancing in black blood.

We didn't try to help him. Whatever that says about us, the thought didn't even enter our heads. Instead, we ran for the shelter of the hospital. Tanya was ahead of me, still holding my hand, and I saw the red dot trace a slash across the back of her T-shirt. But there were no more shots and we made it to the cover of the loading dock. Perhaps the gunman had become entranced by the game he was playing, had been unwilling to reload as that would have meant calling off his red light for a few seconds. That's what probably saved us. That and our cowardice.

The emergency ward opened onto the hospital's lobby, which was cordoned off by a grim line of soldiers sporting identical guns and faces, anonymous and grey. There was some lighting— obviously a hospital would have its own generator— but not much. Every third fixture was working. We emerged into the ER like scriptless extras on a film set. An apt simile, because the Emergency Room was a horror movie.

Nothing especially new here, of course. Every time I've been in an emergency ward I've experienced that horror movie dread, the feeling that something terrible is going to come flailing around the corner at any moment, that every conceivable choice open to you is the wrong one and will lead straight to the gates of Hell.

Why are we even here? I wondered to myself. What on earth did doctors do with broken ribs anyway? You always see bandages wrapped around people's chests in movies, but what does a tight bandage do except push shattered rib shards deeper into the hot and floppy depths of your innards?

We passed a middle-aged man who reeked of rum. He lay on the linoleum wringing himself like a sodden dishcloth, his checked shirt covered in a slimy, clear vomit that puddled beside his head. He smacked his swollen lower lip again and again, opened his eyes wide, then winced in slow motion.

People sat bleeding against the walls, heads bowed, ashamed to be seen leaking, cupping themselves in various ways, thinking clotting thoughts in the absence of medical attention. In front of us, a lone doctor in filthy green scrubs stood screaming at a pimple-faced teen in an Eminem T-shirt. The kid had the dyed-black hair, ragged shag, and scabby face of someone whose problems predated the current crisis. His forehead was a mass of blue and purple bruises; blood trickled down where the skin had ruptured.

'You fucking idiot!' The doctor slapped the boy, who was

trying to stagger past him. He blocked the kid's way and slapped him again, harder. Seeing us, the doctor—a classic A-type—began issuing orders.

'You!' He meant me. 'Hold this piece of shit for me. Every time I leave him alone he goes over to that wall and smashes his head into it.' I saw a stained, cracked spot on the wall where the glossy white paint had been breached. 'Then he falls down and lies there for a few minutes and gets up and does it again. He's already got…You hold him. I've got real patients to see to.'

The doctor stalked off, and I slumped into an empty chair. The boy tried to stumble past Tanya, and she let him. He did what the doctor had said he'd do—smashed his head then fell to his knees and moaned.

Tanya came and sat down next to me. 'What was I going to do? Stand there with my hand up like a school crossing guard until—'

Something stopped her in mid-sentence.

For a moment I thought she was freezing up like Stop Sign Guy had, but that wasn't it. I followed the line of her gaze and saw the most terrible thing in the entire terrible scene. An Indian woman in a sari sat in a bucket chair, expressionless, a small boy on her lap, turned in toward his mother's warmth. One of the woman's arms dangled uselessly at her side, broken or dislocated, while the other was wrapped tight around her son's shoulders. And the boy? He was angel-asleep.

His eyelids swollen, his lashes long and black, his face unguarded and dreaming. Smiling back at us all from wherever he'd gone. And I knew where he'd gone, knew what dream he was having. I could almost see the golden light shining through his forehead right there in the ER.

While I stared, transfixed, Tanya moved. She strode toward the mother, a warning on her lips.

But it was too late. The others had seen him.

Then all I could think was fairy tales, how the world was a wolf, about to swallow that innocent face whole and force it down into its leathery gullet. Slowly, the crowd moved in on mother and child.

The kid with the smashed-in forehead had looked up from his gumbo-lap and seen the Sleeper boy too. Even as Tanya made her move, he'd already staggered to his feet and begun to point and prattle.

'That kid's sleeping! The doctor gave him something to make him sleep!'

Heads turned and everyone in the room began to press around mother and son.

'What did they give him?' a pretty redhead in sandals demanded, clenching and unclenching her fists. 'I want some too! I need some!'

The mother smiled weakly. 'Nothing. They gave him nothing, ma'am. We are here for my arm only.'

'Bullshit!' screamed a man in a pale grey suit, moving toward the pair. 'Just tell us what the doc gave him. We don't want to hurt your kid.'

The very fact of the denial revealed it as a lie, and everyone in the room knew it. You could feel the hesitation as a certain line was reached, then crossed.

'What did the doctor give him? Was it a needle? Check his arm!'

The little boy was awake now. He looked up at his mother's face. Just before the thicket closed him off from my sight, his head pivoted and he looked straight at me, smiling calmly. Like he was reassuring me even as the mob enveloped him.

Then all I could hear was the mother's voice. 'The doctor. I haven't even seen him yet. Please…!'

The doctor arrived back on the scene and forced his way into the thick of the wriggling mass.

'This is completely absurd,' I heard him say, his voice barely audible above the screaming that had now started. 'Believe me, I never—'

Then all we could see was writhing.

And sounds I don't care to try to represent or transcribe: what used to be called the cat's melody. Then the soldiers came rushing in and began firing.

And once more we weren't heroes.

And then a gap, a hole in this manuscript.

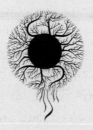

DAY 5
THE BLEEDING OF
A DEAD BODY

It was believed that, at the approach of a murderer,
the blood of the murdered body gushed out.

When I awoke I could somehow tell, despite the lack of any light beyond the dim glow of a battery-powered exit sign, that it was morning. Tanya's arms were wrapped around me, but slackly. She hadn't moved, didn't seem to have blinked, even, all her live-long night.

I closed my eyes and felt every touch I'd ever received come alive on my skin, remnants of my latest dream.

This time I'd been walking down Denman Street with, absurdly enough, an ice cream cone in my hand when the world flung itself apart. Waking up was beyond anticlimax; it was a kind of betrayal. And I felt resentful to be back.

Lying there, I saw the previous night's mother and son in my mind's eye, and behind them the mother and daughter from the Safeway. It's an image that resonates through centuries, between cultures, between species, even. Mother and child, far up Birchin Lane with the longest gauntlet of all to run.

'What are you thinking about?' Tanya asked in a dull voice.

'You don't want to know.'

'Why not?' she asked, suddenly suspicious.

'It's nothing, Medusa. Just…nothing.'

'Stop calling me Medusa, Paul. It makes me sound like a monster. Why can't you call me 'darling' or 'honey' or something normal? Why does everything have to be one of your stupid geeky references?'

I didn't reply, and after a silent while we gathered ourselves together and got going. Crawling out of our hiding place, a jammed together nest of chairs in an empty conference room, we entered the echo-straining silence of an aftermath.

We made for the loading bays, away from the splatted facts of the halls up front. Maybe my ribs weren't broken after all; this morning I could limp a little better, could almost fake a sleep-depraved shamble. Following Tanya down the hallway, I saw a large dark patch on the back of her jeans; during the night, she'd pissed herself. I sniffed myself and winced. Hair and nails growing, skin slowly shedding. We were ridiculous factories, producing smells and oils and shit and piss. Better things went into us than ever came out.

'There were footsteps all night. People kept running past. Guns. God, all sorts of horrible sounds. I can't believe you slept through it,' she added spitefully, as angry at the word 'slept' as she was at me.

I didn't reply, didn't feel fully tethered to Tanya's ragged world. Rather, I felt like a slowly-inflating balloon, tugged at by clean winds. But what would come of it? Would I eventually bulk up to God-size, or would Death creep in, pin in hand, and burst my bubble?

We emerged into chill light, shading our eyes, and saw how, overnight, new structures had risen alongside Vancouver's green glass towers. We wouldn't have been able to see this new architecture with our old eyes, mind you: we saw them with our new ones. Sharp white spires of thought, thin as needles, pierced the sky, pierced everything on the ground. All my precious orphan Nod-words were crawling closer, each with their own particular, pressing agenda: chokepear, chatterpie. Yesterday's Blemmye had only been the herald of this new world, a Silver Surfer to the slowly-advancing Galactus whose gargantuan form was drawing nearer and nearer to our blue sky.

'Tanya, I…'

But that's all I said. In the time it took those two words to leave my mouth, I grew sick of my voice, physically ill from intent.

A billion miles over to my right, Tanya didn't seem to have noticed that I'd spoken at all. In the sunlight, the skin around her eyes was cracked and dry as a riverbed. She scowled at me, then quickly turned away. I pictured middle-aged couples with nothing left to say to one another but with years and years of life left to live out, sitting in shamed and furious silence beside one another. In restaurants, in cars, on holiday beaches.

When we were about halfway back to our apartment, we came upon a crowd surrounding a woman standing atop a concrete bench in the middle of one of those tiny roundabouts the city installed back in the 1980s to slow traffic and dissuade johns from cruising for hookers.

'I know how to sleep!' the woman cried. 'I know!'

She was in her forties, with the look of someone grown thin and old waiting for something that she'd known all along was never really going to come her way. Even if nothing was coming, you still had to wait: those were the rules. And if you were waiting anyway, you inevitably ended up pretending that your vigil wasn't really in vain. To salvage a little dignity. And besides, maybe if you faked it long enough, you'd get lucky and hope would pop up like a morning mushroom on a dewy morning, suddenly whole and instantly there. No one could really say it was impossible, not really. No one knew for sure.

Anyway, this woman had grown tired long before the world ended: I could see it in her anonymous hair colour, in the way her jeans fit, in the list of her shoulders.

Her audience pressed close, trampling the ranks of city tulips festooning the roundabout.

'I know how!'

No one believed she knew anything. Her eyes were too red

and raw for her to be in possession of some magical sleep recipe, but the crowd seemed willing, for now, to go along with the charade. With TV over, they were here for the freak show.

She swept out a knife and held it high. I looked around for a cop, but we hadn't seen one all morning. Just an abandoned uniform in a heap on a bench.

'This is how!' she cried, then took the long thin blade, held it toward her wide open right eye with one hand, then reached out and slammed the palm of her other hand into its base, driving the blade in to the hilt.

The crowd dilated spasmodically as the woman fell, a dropped doll.

What was left laying there mid-roundabout *did* look a lot like sleep. She lay on her back, the smooth wooden handle of the knife pointing straight up from her face like the gnomon on a sundial. No blood just yet, just a little clear liquid running down one cheek like a tear. Soon ravens would come and be unkind to her.

The crowd kept spreading; I grabbed Tanya's arm and pulled her along as fast as I could manage, trying to stay ahead of its thinning perimeter.

'I won't tell anyone, Paul,' she announced suddenly, in a tattletale voice. And then she was angry. 'Don't be so fucking paranoid!'

Several stragglers looked our way, but we looked mad enough together, and any kindling suspicions soon evaporated.

* * *

A block from our apartment, two blocks from Stanley Park, a shocking sight. Five children stood clustered together on the sidewalk. Children like from before, not like the ones we'd seen all morning lurking in alleys, crouched and lidless with terror. These ones were smiling, just like the boy in the ER and the little girl behind the Safeway. A little grubby, but otherwise they appeared unaffected by the chaos.

Tanya and I stopped in our tracks, like record player needles when a late-afternoon storm hits and the power goes out. In the ensuing silence, the children nudged one another.

'Who are they?' Tanya asked in wonder, briefly emerging from her fog.

'I've no idea.'

The oldest was a girl of around ten who wore a T-shirt and pink shorts. The youngest was a boy with longish blonde bangs who couldn't have been more than two. He held the older girl's hand and stared shyly at me. These were fellow Sleepers, clear-eyed and unconcerned. As we stood facing one another in our aquarium of silence, the oldest girl kept looking toward a row of shrubs that stood outside a stucco Vancouver-as-California condominium complex.

I cleared my throat.

'Are you okay?'

The other four looked to the oldest girl, who stared at me for them all.

'Can I—?' I began, but they turned and ran, fluttering down the sidewalk toward the park and the slow-waving willows that ringed the perimeter.

Across the street, a young man with no shirt and tangled black hair raised a quivering arm in the direction of the children's flight, looked in our direction, and opened his mouth silently. Then he turned and began to plod after them, but much too slowly to ever catch up.

Then a sound from behind the scraggly row of shrubs that had attracted the children's attention: giggling.

The little girl we discovered playing hide-and-seek behind the shrubs wouldn't tell us her name; like the other children, she either couldn't or wouldn't speak. She wasn't silent in a war-traumatized way, but in a shrugging, nothing-much-to-say manner. A pretty little thing, around four years old, with blonde hair and a wide brow—Alice In Wonderland-ish. She returned our smiles and didn't flinch from Tanya's touch when she picked her up.

When we got her home, placed her on the couch and began to pelt her with questions, she simply replied with a bemused tilt of her head. It was as though our enquiries about names and the whereabouts of mommies and daddies weren't quite up to snuff, but she was too well-mannered to tell us.

We called her Zoe, Tanya having plucked the name from a mental list of future-children names that women seem to carry around inside themselves like eggs. Women. Eggs in their bodies, babies in their eyes.

From the moment we'd peered over the hedge and seen Zoe bouncing a small pink ball on the fractured concrete, Tanya had taken fevered possession of her. She scooped her up and marched the final block to our apartment without waiting for me. As I followed, Zoe watched me, her round face bobbing sombrely on Tanya's left shoulder. The feeling that we were living out our lives together in fast forward was intensified by our sudden acquisition of a foster child.

'Well, if you won't speak, little missy, maybe you'll eat!' Tanya said, a little too brightly, her haggard face working up to a smile.

She emptied the cupboards, lining up our twin jars of tahini, a jumbo box of Corn Flakes, dandruff-y carrots, bread, and apples on the breakfast bar. The child hopped off the couch, ambled over, and picked up the box of cereal which she proceeded to shake like a giant, ungainly maraca.

'So you like Corn Flakes, do you?' Tanya asked, then headed over to the fridge and removed our last jug of milk. She opened it and sniffed, screwed up her face in disgust, then brought out a box of granola bars instead.

As Zoe munched away happily, Tanya came and sat down beside me. I put my arm around her. She flinched and began to pull away, but then something changed and she snuggled in toward me.

'It's almost like she's ours, Paul.'

'Almost,' I replied, not liking the direction Tanya was taking this.

'Do you think we would have had a family?'

'Don't say "would have".'

She sighed in exasperation but didn't pull away. 'I don't know if we would have. Do you think we would have stayed together and got married?'

'I would have married you, even if I had to do it on my own.' It was a feeble attempt at wit, but it worked. She giggled and swung her legs up onto my lap.

'Maybe I would have married you. You're pretty cute. Especially when you're being all serious and writerly. That's when you're at your silliest, Paul. Do you know that?'

'Now I know you're going crazy.'

Tanya leaned in and gave me a hot kiss under my jaw, on my jugular.

'I love you.'

'Love you too, Paul. You would have been worth marrying. Me not so much, maybe.'

'Don't be—' but she hushed me and we sat together in silence as Zoe, our truncated hypothetical future, munched away. That was the last real conversation we ever had, and I'll take it with me as far down this road as I end up travelling.

When it got dark, we lit candles. They didn't help the weirded-out atmosphere. Coupled with the screaming and smashing sounds from out on the streets, the twitchy yellow light only served to make our apartment seem like the den of some urban Satanist. When she could wriggle free of Tanya's hugging arms for a few minutes, Zoe entertained herself by silently wafting her hands back and forth across the flames. Eventually we managed to persuade Zoe to blow out the candles and two thirds of us called it a night. Tanya put Zoe to sleep in our bed, I crashed on the sofa, while Tanya sat in the dark and waited for dawn.

At about four in the morning I was awakened by the sound of someone shouldering the front door. I ran out into the hall and found Tanya already there, flat against the wall with our longest, pointiest kitchen knife clutched in her right hand. We stood there for a few moments until the banging stopped. Voices were raised in dispute, something got slammed on the ground, then footsteps and hawing voices echoed down the hall.

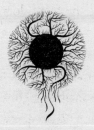

DAY 6
THE ADMIRAL OF THE BLUE

A butcher who dresses in blue to conceal blood-stains.

At dawn, the sky cracked open and daylight spilled all over our ravaged City of Destruction. Armless birdsong, audible through closed windows, made the worm of devastation even harder to swallow.

A strangely domestic scene that morning. Tanya was her old self, or might have appeared so to a casual observer. Like an alcoholic hot on the trail of some new resolve, she'd washed and applied makeup and was cheerfully tending to Zoe's needs, washing and cleaning, playing and feeding, all the while chatting to me or speaking to the silent child in a high, girlish voice, the kind of tone people who aren't good with kids use when trying to be good with kids. The kind of voice I always suspect kids can see through. Was Tanya good with kids? I had no idea. Even though we'd been together for over three years, our shared moments around the young had been limited to brief encounters with colleagues' offspring as they were introduced at dinner parties or barbeques before being shuffled back off to their segregated kiddie-kingdoms.

Zoe didn't seem to mind, seemed to assume that she and Tanya were just playing a pickup game of mother-daughter pretend. But Tanya wasn't playing: she was brushing Zoe's hair in deadly earnest: gentle with the tangles but obviously fighting the urge to pull and tear. For my part, I sat on the couch and kept watch in case she lost it.

What must it have been like, I wonder now, to have been the only person in the room that morning taking their role in our pretend family seriously? On some level, Tanya must have known that Zoe wasn't really charmed by her exertions, and that I wasn't really onside. On some level, it must have really hurt.

'Paul?'

'Yeah?'

'We should take Zoe out for breakfast when I've done with her hair. Show her our Breakfastery-That-Must-Remain-Nameless.'

'I don't think that's doable, Tanya.'

She slapped her cheek, shook her head and laughed. 'Oh, right. Wow. Of course not. Christ.' Then, without missing a beat, 'So what do you have going on today?'

'We should try to find Zoe's parents, but I haven't got a clue how to go about it if she's not going to talk to us.'

'Parents?'

As though on cue, Zoe turned and smiled through me, then

went back to brushing the stuffed grizzly bear Tanya had given her the night before, retrieved from a small stash of childhood stuffies she kept in the bedroom closet. Tanya brushing Zoe brushing the grizzly.

After a while she put down her hairbrush and smiled. 'Paul? You know what I just remembered?'

'What?'

'That time we went river rafting at Hell's Gate? Remember how we were pretending to be so nervous? You said you wondered if it really was the gate to Hell and when we came out on the other end we were there, even if everything looked like normal?'

'Remember the drive home?'

She left Zoe to her bear and came and snuggled up, rubbing her bristly left calf against my thigh.

'We passed the Hell Shell gas station…'

'And the Denny's of the Damned and the Infernal Ikea. I remember.'

'That was a really fun day.'

'A hell of a day.'

She looked briefly at me, then down at her lap, her smile fading. My arm was around her shoulder, but I could feel her grow distant again and soon enough she wriggled free and went back over to Zoe and resumed brushing.

I turned on my laptop. (charge remaining: 18%) and tried to locate a network. No luck. A laptop is a pretty stupid thing to own when the Web is down. I could have played Minesweeper or tapped away at my manuscript until the battery gave out, I suppose, but those were the sum total of my options. Beyond that, my almost-new $3000 MacBook Air might have functioned— very briefly—as a campfire waffle iron or a fairly lame frisbee.

I tried to make eye contact with Tanya, but she glared at me, hundred-proof hatred pouring from her eyes. So while her unsteady hands plied Zoe with dry Corn Flakes and brownish apple slices, I sat straight-legged on the balcony in a sliver of sun and tried to make my thoughts make sense. Tried to *make sense*; tried to manufacture it. My head a little factory, chug-chug-chugging away.

How to break down what was happening? Some children were sleeping, some weren't. Same for the grownups. The non-Sleepers, child and adult alike, were straightforward in their blossoming psychoses. But there was clearly a difference between the way child and adult Sleepers were handling things.

I, for example, was at least somewhat disturbed by the murder and mayhem I was seeing. And I was more than a little put out by the thought, for example, of Tanya's swelling madness and seemingly inevitable demise. But Zoe didn't appear to notice what was going on. She was young, but not so young that she shouldn't be scared. In fact, her normalcy was starting to freak me out.

Of course, I wasn't completely right in my own head. First off, there was the Dream. Sheepishly, I dub it 'the Dream': 'The Dream of the Golden Light' sounds like something cheesy from the annals of Chinese folklore or the ramblings of some wake-and-bake New Age guru. Granted, 'The Dream' sounds a little pretentious, but what other options do I have? And you can't say, given the circumstances, that it doesn't warrant capitalization. Just count yourself lucky that I don't call it THE DREAM in hysterical all caps. What can I say? Sometimes language just lets us down.

In the Dream, nothing bothered me, like nothing seemed to bother Zoe when she was awake. Did that perhaps mean that she and the other children like her were living in the Dream full time? It was a thought to keep in mind.

Earlier, I'd found a pad of legal paper shoved under a cushion on the couch. Tanya's TV notes, transcribed straight from the mouths of the Brazen Heads:

Night 6

Symptoms of depersonalization occur and a clear sense of identity is lost. This is called sleep deprivation psychosis. The effects of sleep deprivation are more psychological than physical. Reflexes are impaired but heart rate, respiration, blood pressure and body temperature show very little change. The main physical consequences seem to be hand tremors, droopy eyelids, problems in focusing the eyes and a heightened sensitivity to pain.

So. Something to look forward to.

'Paul!'

Inside, Tanya was rocking back and forth on the couch, oblivious Zoe pressed tight to her hip.

'We haven't got any milk, Paul. This child needs milk.'

'The power's out. The milk will have all gone sour.'

She sneered as she mimicked me. '*The milk will all be sour*'. Jesus Christ, Paul, use that big fucking brain you're so proud of. There's going to be shelf milk in the stores.'

'But the stores are all...'

'So, what? We're just going to sit here and let Zoe die of thirst? Is that your big plan, Paul?'

Instead of replying, I gazed into the calm sky of Zoe's face. There's something holy about the face of a child weathering adult storms; I remember this from my own youth. Squabbles over bills and vacation plans; the uptight soccer dads and chain-smoking moms to whom my peers and I somehow belonged. Up to a certain age, kids can't engage the grown up madness around them even if they try. They don't have the chops yet; all they can do is watch and wait.

While we bickered, Zoe turned her head toward the door, perhaps thinking about making a run for it. Tanya looked at me then triangulated her way down to Zoe. Then she looked back up at me, and her rheumy eyes were filled with tears. She blinked them away and held the child tight, stroking her hair. I can't say if the stroking persuaded Zoe to stay with us and not flee our mom and pop Bedlam for the Big Box Bedlam outside, but Tanya's affectionate arm appeared to play at least a small part in Zoe's willingness to remain.

Sensing this, Tanya quickly swampwatered her way into the role of the meek and mild hausfrau.

'I don't want to fight. We just need something for Zoe to drink.'

'Okay. I'll see what I can do.'

I went into the kitchen and grabbed the scariest-looking

knife on the premises—the same one Tanya had used last night. Concealing it beneath my shirt, I went into the front hall and opened the door. Then proceeded to reel.

Someone had spray-painted three neon pink words, in all jagged caps, on the opposite wall:

WELCOME TO NOD

Not exactly the font or colour I'd have chosen for my imagined dust jacket, but there you go.

When Tanya didn't hear the door close and lock behind me, she came to investigate.

'What the *fuck*? Did you do this, Paul?'

I didn't reply.

'Well, who did?'

Zoe came up behind us, and Tanya shooed her back into the living room.

'I don't know...'

'This is from your book, Paul. Your stupid book. Whoever did this has read your stuff. Who's read your manuscript? Think!'

'No one. Just you.'

'That's impossible!'

For a moment I found myself wondering if this graffiti was Tanya's work, but quickly dismissed the idea. Her outrage was too savage to be a sham. Think. The book I'd planned to call *Nod* had been too embryonic to share with anyone besides Tanya. It had seemed a little too poetic and whimsical to run by any of my online colleagues in what we called the Weird Word World.

Tanya let loose a sputtering chain of 'fuck's, shaking her head as she spattered them on the carpet, left and right.

I looked from her to my thoughts made flesh, and then went out to try to find some shelf milk. Emerging, empty-handed, from the third smashed-in store I'd attempted to plunder that morning, I began to understand all the teacher-talk from my youth about the Importance of Liquids to the Survival of the Human Species. Back at the apartment the water was off and we were down to a couple of litres of Coke and two tetra packs of apple juice.

A ragged man and woman stood on the sidewalk at the far end of the block, whispering to one another over a plastic shopping bag. They kept sneaking looks in my direction. Everybody I'd seen since leaving home looked like they were carrying an invisible case of nitro-glycerine in their shaking hands. Both dangerous *and* in danger. Suicide bombers must have felt like this. When I stepped onto their stretch of sidewalk, the couple panicked and ran, dropping the bag. I went up and looked into it and saw the body of a tiny blue baby that couldn't have been more than a week or two old. The woman, presumably the poor thing's mother, was peering at me from behind a doorway further down the block, hissing. I crossed the street and kept moving.

Soon after, I saw a guy who jogged the same Seawall route as me coming out of an apartment building. I didn't know him well, but we'd chatted a few times. I raised my arm to wave, but when he saw me he turned on his heel and hurried back inside.

One block further, in front of an elementary school, forty or so people stood in a circle on kid-pounded grass. Someone in the centre of the group was speaking in a low monotone, too far away for me to be able to make out the words. I was intrigued: this was the most orderly scene I'd come across since my trip to the Safeway a couple of days ago. Crouching behind a mailbox I watched, trying to imagine what could make a group of forty sleep-deprived Vancouverites so quiet and attentive. Then, right behind me, someone spoke in a shrill, threatening voice.

'Where's my pillow? Where'd you hide my goddamn pillow!?'

I didn't have his pillow. That wasn't good news.

I spun around and faced my accuser's scabbed and hairy-scary shins.

'Give me my fucking *pillow*!'

Then, for a while, nothing.

Someone's shirt was wadded under my throbbing head, and a steady circle of faces stared down at me, their lips gnawed raw and their eyes abandoned. Behind them the sky. When I tried to sit up, they scattered, as though afraid. After a while they moved closer again, forming a whispering ring around me.

'What's going on?'

No response.

I staggered to my feet, thinking fast, hoping against hope to create some fellow-feeling.

'Did you get the asshole who hit me?'

Still no reply. At the front of the group, a woman in filthy jeans scratched her crotch vigorously, like she was grating cheese. Too dizzy to make a run for it, I started to slowly back away, praying that the circle would break and let me pass. One step, two. Then I bumped into someone standing behind me, blocking my retreat. I turned and saw him.

Charles.

He was dressed all in blue. Sky blue shirt, baby blue slacks, medieval Catholic blue shoes, fresh from some plundered boutique—all the while exuding his customary raw red welcome. I couldn't take my eyes of the sharp cuffs of his sleeves and his crisp shirt collar. Possessions no longer existed in the old way. As in the case of any catastrophe, things were now just lying around waiting to be picked up. But how to keep them? That would be the new problem that would now replace the old one of acquisition.

Charles pulled a greasy, thumb-damp wad of paper from his back pocket and held it in front of my face. It was the printout of *Nod* Tanya and I had taken to breakfast five long mornings ago. And then, too late to do me any good, it all clicked into place: motive, opportunity, and madness. Of course.

'Welcome to Nod, Paul,' he said. 'Welcome to the dream you've brought us.' And then louder, to the group, 'Welcome home to your own people, teacher.'

'What's going on?' I hissed.

He smiled and kept talking.

'Can you hear the humility?' He turned and addressed the

crowd. 'Didn't I tell you he'd be humble? That when he came he'd be humble for us? Blemmyes and banshees, no fear! Oh, the devil is out there, roaming between the tipping skyscrapers, dressed as a monk and looking for souls, but no fear! This man can spot the devil from a mile away! Evil Rat and his army are out there, but this man will conjure them away!'

Several people began to dart frightened looks around. Others sneered, but nervously, if you can imagine that. This was a crowd on the verge of some big decision with heavy implications for both Charles and me.

'Tell us the plan,' the crotch-grating woman demanded. Less than a week ago she'd been a high-end soccer mom: her blondeness was still relatively intact, and her voice still sounded accustomed to being heard.

Charles grabbed my arm and began to lead me toward the school. The urgency of his tugging told me what I already suspected: he wasn't the master of this group, only its provisional leader. Eyes glowered as we began to move away.

'Soon! I need to show Paul the temple first. Then he'll speak to you! Just wait here!'

And they stayed put, though their blood surged toward us.

'What's happening, Charles?' I whispered as we entered the school.

The foyer was dim, though the pocked linoleum glared in black, refracted sunlight.

He was giggling. 'It's all coming true, Paul. All of it. Just like you wrote.'

'Like I wrote?'

He started playing sly. 'You know. All the old words are waking up and rubbing their eyes! The Church Invisible is becoming the Church Visible. Now that sleep is finally over.' He was quoting my own words back at me, distorted through the funhouse mirror of his mind.

'You think that I…? That's—' I was going to say 'crazy' but reconsidered.

'The businessman! While the businessman guzzles his martini, Paul—I really shouldn't have to be telling you this—while he guzzles, he tells his friends in the bar that it's all a game. The way he makes his money, I mean. He tells them that while the poor parade on by, outside in the freezing cold. The windows are steamed, Paul, and he can't see outside and they can't see in. It's Christmas, and he makes us all swallow the contradiction, forces it down our throats. He tells his friends that trading stocks and making money is all a game. But is it? To him? Does he even know what a game is? And what about a little boy being forced to eat broccoli that's been boiled so long he can strain it through his teeth? Is that a game? Does he know? Do you see?'

I didn't. Instead, I thought of Tanya and Zoe all alone back in the apartment and felt the school's walls press in on me. How stupid we'd been to remain in the city this long. All I could think to do was keep him talking and look for an opportunity to make a run for it.

'I don't understand. Can you explain?'

By feigning interest, I ran the risk of sounding patronizing, but I couldn't think what else to do.

'Glad to, Paul. What's real? What's fake? Is what we intend to do ever what we *really* want to do? And if not, can it matter?' He laughed. 'I can see I'm losing you, Paul. I'll try again.' He slapped my rolled up manuscript against his thigh. 'You wrote this book, right?'

'I'm—I was writing it.'

'And this book explicates the things I'm seeing, that we're all seeing and thinking. Colours are bleeding. Spirits are flashing past. You know all this.'

I thought of the Blemmye from the other evening and felt my ribs creak in rhythm to my throbbing head, my throbbing fucking universe.

'But how can it do that? It's just a book, for Christ's sake.'

Now that I was asking a real question, Charles got angry. He snarled, keeping his words on a short tether. 'It's not just a book! Of course it's not. They're not just words. It's a map. All these words have been hidden away and now they're coming back to the main stage, Paul. You're a prophet, Paul.'

Each time he said my name I found myself grinding my teeth.

'But the question is, 'how did you know?' How did you prognosticate it, Paul?'

Charles loved big words, loved forcing them into his sentences no matter how much they squealed.

All around us, glass cases on the walls were filled with student drawings and papier-mâché sculptures. Every piece of kiddie art looked as insane and distorted as anything I'd seen outside or written about in *Nod*. Charles caught me staring and smiled even more widely, until I began to fear his face would split from the strain.

'I noticed it too. All those grotesque heads and jagged lines. And just a week ago, just think of it, Paul—all those adults smiling so condescendingly because they thought their kids were too stupid to get reality right. Oops. What do you think?'

He waited while I thought fast. What did I have to say to get away from him and his greasy mob? One thing was clear: to refuse to play the part he had written for me would probably be to invite more danger than I'd be able to handle. So I started making things up.

'I don't know. I guess I was fascinated by what's buried beneath, by what was buried beneath the old reality. Sometimes I felt like those words were more real than the world around me. But I don't know what…'

I'd run out of words. Faces peered through the glass in the skinny windows beside the doors—trees behind them, shaking their fists at the sky.

'The folks out there want to come in and see you, but I don't think you're ready to meet them yet. Let me make this easy for you, Paul. Okay?'

I bowed my head.

'Just ask me what you can do to help.'

'What can I do to help, Charles?'

He clapped his hands, and I jumped.

'We've got to get organized, Paul. It's all a piece of shit. Just think of me as the martini man, sipping away. It's all shit but not *really*. Understand? Well, you will. We need a guide, Paul.

A leader, a figurehead, a guru, a plaster saint. We gotta get *organizized*. Did you ever see *Taxi Driver*? Robert DeNiro? You should. Have. It's gone for good now. No more movies, ever. Hah! People are staggering around out there, smacking each other on the heads with bricks, Paul. It's ridiculous. It's embarrassing for the species! Who's insane? That's insane. People aren't insane: it's the things they do that are crazy. Clearly, clearly, clearly. So we need to make some sense here. 'What we can't change has to be a church', Paul. Get it? We have to enshrine you because your book makes sense. It makes sense to me, Paul. Christ, I was up all night reading it when I got it the other day. That's not as impressive a statement as it once was, I'll admit that into evidence, but still! There were other things I could have been doing. Lots of other things we need to do. So let's talk turkey.'

'What do you mean?'

'Turkey!' He grinned wildly into my face.

I laughed with no hope in my heart. Now I was seeing both the name of the game and my role in it. Forget Rice Christian, Charles planned to set me up as a Rice Jesus. He'd been a little cracked before all this, which presumably meant he was two steps ahead in this new reality. When the world stops its rotation and begins to spin backwards, I suppose, stragglers suddenly find themselves ahead of the pack. It must have been quite a feeling.

'Okay. Now that's out of the way, let's talk what comes next. Next you need to go out there with me, tell those poor saps that you'll guide them through these changes, help them to live in Nod.'

'But I…'

'Do you really think you 'just' wrote that book, Paul? Is your self-esteem really that low? Do you really think that, prior to seeing that burning bush in the desert, Moses thought he'd see a fucking burning bush in the desert? Or do you think that Moses was a fucking nutbar, Paul? And what about the civilizations that grew out of that encounter between that nutbar and that nutbush? Were they nutbar civilizations? Can you answer that? We won't even go into Jesus. Christ! These things, they happen. Nobody knows who or why or where or when. Things just happen, Paul. I mean, can't you see that, Paul?' He threw his arms out. 'Isn't it obvious? So let's just accept that things are happening. Okay? As a start.'

Charles' left foot tapped out a double time beat.

'Okay.'

'Good. Now, here's what's going to happen next. We're going to go out there and do a meet and greet. I'll do most of the talking. You just look mysterious and…and potent, okay? Impotent if you can swing it! Just kidding! All you need to know is this: being Awake is a gift from God. It's the next step forward. It's allowing us to see the bigger universe. And that expanded universe can be a scary place. Be compassionate. But we need to be worthy of this opportunity, right? Worthy. There have been reports of monsters already, Paul. Monsters on the edge of people's vision. Bat creatures and walking trees. We can name them and that way we can own them like Adam did in Eden. Right? Nod, right? But some other reports, too. Of creatures making contact. *Bloody Bones* is out there. You remember him, right? And *Bloody Hands*. All in the streets, Paul, scraping around. And you and I are going to help the people out there deal with these demons, Paul. We're going to get comfortable with the New World Order.'

'I don't know if I'll know what to say, Charles.'

But his words blazed right on past mine. I was reminded of firestorms that sucked all the oxygen out of a place. In a forest, after one of these, firefighters would find deer and other animals, still standing, burned to charcoal.

'And then we'll go to that apartment of yours and get you your girlies and bring them here to the school, which will be our cathedral for the next few days. Then bigger digs. And food. After all, little Zoe needs milk, right? Even shelf milk will do. Right, Paul?'

My heart stopped.

'Shelf milk. Ha. That's right. We've been watching over you for the last two nights, Paul. If not for my sentries, you'd have been beaten to death in your sleep by some of the more confused people out there. They're going from door to door, Paul, offering mischief. Doing crazy shit. Bat shit crazy. Chugging little nonsense factories, right? But we'll straighten them out, don't sweat it.'

'I don't know what you're talking about,' I said feebly.

'Don't lie to me, Paul; I'm not green in the eye. The walls have ears and eyes and even fingers. Glory holes. The walls have cocks now and it's easy to find yourself *fucked* when your back's to the wall. Ha! Now listen.' He dropped his voice and became sober. 'I can tell that you're a Sleeper, which is problematic. I can't make sense of that yet. But we'll deal with it at a later date. For now, just get with the program. You're going to have to do some things. Restrict your sleep! Have some sense of decorum! Get some bags going beneath those eyes! What are you thinking, walking around in this fucking mess so daisy fresh and fragrant, Paul?'

Charles leaned toward me and sniffed. Then he clapped his hand on my shoulder and pushed me toward the door and those faces pressed against the glass.

'And one more thing. A little thing but a big one. Stop Charles-ing me. Don't call me Charles anymore. I'm the Admiral of the Blue now. Cheesy, I know. But what the fuck, eh?'

And then he pushed the doors wide open. The light poured in. The crowd splashed backward, then pooled, then slowly crept toward me.

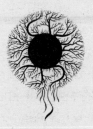

DAY 7
TOMORROW NEVER COMES

A reproof to those who defer till to-morrow
what should be done to-day.

I'd taken Charles' advice and only slept around two hours the previous night, sat up reading through old magazines by candlelight while Tanya ignored me, staring at some book hour after hour without turning a page.

Now, in the early morning light, it was almost showtime. While Zoe watched from the sofa, hands clasped beneath her chin, Tanya smeared eye shadow under my cheekbones in an attempt to make me look even more haggard than I already felt. She giggled furiously—like a fury—but when her task was complete, she fell back, mouth slack, eyes dull. I tried to snap her out of it.

'How do I look?'

She chomped her mouth shut and pinched herself hard, something she'd taken to doing during the last twenty four hours. Her forearms were mottled with black and blue niblets of pain.

'It's just you. You in makeup.'

Those were the first words she'd addressed to me in over twelve hours. And even now she was speaking, not to me, not at me, but through me. It was as if we'd been married for fifty years and I was visiting her in the Alzheimer's ward with not our daughter, but our granddaughter.

I recall a passage from *Being and Nothingness,* a portly little tome I'd forced myself to read one summer as an overly earnest undergraduate. About the only thing I remember from its six hundred-odd pages was when Sartre, expanding on Descartes, wrote that the reason we know others exist is because when they look at us, we feel *looked at*. He called the entity that was staring back at us the Other. From that meeting of the eyes, everything else in our fragile human universes blossomed forth. But! Think of how easily human status is taken away—by war, by hospitals, by arguments about whose turn it is to take out the recycling. How easily we can turn people into things. And now Tanya had turned me into a thing.

My heart ached at the separation I felt, but I swallowed down the pain as best I could, not wanting to upset any of the three children in the room: oblivious Zoe, the little boy in me who didn't understand what was happening, or the deranged toddler who crouched, teeth bared, behind Tanya's face.

* * *

Yesterday, Charles and a couple of his zombies had accompanied me back to the apartment then left, promising to return for us in the morning. But late at night I heard movement in Mrs Simmons' apartment. Knowing it was Charles' people didn't make me feel any better.

Creepy-crawly. There's a word of fairly modern derivation. From 1968, although it sounds like it could have come from centuries earlier, straight from the pages of Brewer. Charles Manson and his Family, prior to the Tate-La Bianca murders, would sneak into wealthy homes high up in the Hollywood Hills. Late at night, while the owners slept, they'd tiptoe around in the dark, moving things. Rearranging furniture. Pocketing a few items. And then they'd leave, before dawn. Practicing.

The situational irony of my own Admiral of the Blue sharing a Christian name with the head of the Manson Family wasn't lost on me. Was Manson a product of the twentieth century or a sleeper agent from an earlier one? Or was he a time traveller vomited up from some nightmare future? Or were centuries and eras merely convenient but artificial categories we created to render 'reality' manageable through cowering consensus? In that light, a Charles Manson wasn't an aberration so much as a frightening reminder about what lay beneath things, ready to pop up and yell 'Boo!' at any time.

There's an old English phrase that means roughly the same thing: *Miching Malicho.* Even though you've almost certainly never heard it before, you can probably sense the phrase's general meaning from sound alone. *Miching*: a crimped, furtive verb. *Malicho*: a virtual portmanteau inversion of "Draco Malfoy" from the *Harry Potter* books. And that's what it means: a furtive doer of bad deeds. Our language is so laden with associations that writers can easily cough up names pre-loaded with portent. Darth Vader, Uriah Heep, Gollum.

I could see the heroic efforts that Tanya's trembling hand was making. For Zoe's sake. Tanya had emerged from her state of near-catatonia, pulled her hair into a greasy ponytail, and grown suddenly talkative.

'I love this child.'

'I can see that.'

'And she could be any child. That's the point. I could love any child, and by loving my Zoe, I love every child. That's lucky, Paul. I feel really lucky.'

'That's great.'

Her face was finally paying the full price for a week without sleep and showers. As I've already noted, her mouth now had a tendency to droop open when not in use. Her head hung as though on a coat hanger, and when she looked up, she always seemed to be looking at me over the rims of invisible reading glasses. And she had started sniffling away at some sort of cold. God know what sorts of diseases were flying around out there as overstressed immune systems began to crash and burn.

It was all I could do to look at her, honestly. All I could do not to burst into tears and run out of the room.

'Why you and not me, Paul? Is there a reason? If you're chosen, you must know the reason.'

'There's no reason.'

Was there a reason?

'Yes there is. There's always a reason for everything. Tell me.'

Maybe there was a reason.

'No. It's always been this way—random. Why did you and I have food to eat and safe beds to sleep in when we were kids, while the kid next door got abused and the kids in Africa starved?'

She flinched, then placed her mascara wand on the coffee table and held a mirror up to my face.

'Welcome to my world.'

I looked and found myself ridiculous—an extra from an Eighties Hair Metal video. Or so I would have seemed to someone with a good night's sleep under their belt. To the people wandering around outside, I probably just looked par for the course.

'It's time to get going.'

'Where are we going?'

The deal I'd cut with Charles was that the three of us would move into the school today. His followers had been busily boarding up the main floor windows, fortifying the place. That was the deal. In reality we intended to do no such thing.

'North.'

'To the North Pole? Are we going to seek refuge at Santa's place?'

'We'll find some millionaire's place in North Van and take it over. Live like kings.'

She put her hand on my cheek but avoided my eyes.

'There's nowhere to go that isn't here, Paul.'

'You want Zoe to be safe, don't you?'

She paused.

'Yes.'

It was said about Vancouver that once you went beyond five-kilometre-deep North Vancouver, that was it: that was the end of 'civilized' North America. After leaving North Van, you could walk straight to the Arctic Circle and never see a soul or a settlement. This couldn't be literally true: you'd have to cross the occasional forlorn highway or encounter a string or two of hydro lines, but the point still held. Maybe we'd hole up in that imaginary mansion for a few days, then try our luck with the bears and cougars. Maybe if we got far enough away from the city, the curse would lift.

'We can't stay here. It's getting really scary out there.'

'We've seen the writing on the wall,' she snickered to herself.

I hadn't told Tanya anything about Charles and his creepy crawlies. I didn't think she'd have been able to handle the news. Better just to run.

We crammed what little food we had left into a backpack along with some toilet paper and our toothbrushes and slipped out of the apartment as silently as we could, leaving the door ajar as closing it might have alerted the sentries next door.

The air stank as we felt our way down the dark hallway to the stairs. Shameful though it is to say, we'd been using the empty apartment across the hall as a toilet, shitting into a bucket in one of the bedrooms, then dumping the contents out the window into the alley.

There were other smells wafting through the halls, the strongest emanating from Mrs Simmons' place. A puke-up-your-guts sweetness that made us scurry through the darkness, we three blind mice, as fast as we could.

It had felt crafty to plan our escape for five in the morning, before Charles' people returned, though I was fully aware that whoever was watching us wasn't likely to be sleeping on the job. Tanya had made a shawl for Zoe to hide her face from rheumy eyes.

I'd decided we'd walk along the edge of Stanley Park until we got to the causeway that cut through its heart to Lion's Gate Bridge and the North Shore. If trouble approached us from the city, we could always, I reasoned, make a run for it into the rainforest.

It seemed a curious piece of luck that Vancouver was the only major city I knew of with a largely-untouched primordial forest right downtown. Stanley Park was so large, in fact, that it had historically been a refuge for the homeless and the addicted. There were rumoured to be settlements deep in the heart of the park where those unable to afford their own sliver of green glass could take shelter beneath green trees, beyond the green world of money. But did that mean that the woods were now filled with psychotic hobos? No matter. I liked our chances of escape better in the forest.

As we walked, I swung an iron barbell, denuded of weights. The barbell's heft transferred confidence into my right arm, and I did my best to carry it with swaggering ease, mindful of eyes that might be watching our progress. My ribs were feeling a little better today, sore but not so rickety.

As we walked along the goose shit bespattered edge of Lost

Lagoon, a pack of dogs on the far shore snapped at a swan that alternately flew at them, beating its massive wings, then retreated into the water where it paddled in lunatic circles, honking. It was like all of them were engaged in some sort of co-dependent role-playing game: dog and swan playing cat and mouse.

But where were the human beings? Surprisingly for a city with a population of four million, the West End, Vancouver's downtown core, was a mere forty thousand or so. The rest of that four million were commuters from the surrounding areas who filled the city each dawn, then staggered out twenty hours later when the last bars closed. Most likely, everyone who didn't live here had simply gone home to the burbs when things began to fall apart.

I'd seen a few bodies, smelled a few more, but it seemed as though most of us were still alive. So where was everyone? I looked up at the massed ranks of the apartment buildings fronting the park and felt them stare back—hard. Suddenly, our progress felt ant-slow.

'Faster.'

Tanya said nothing, but adjusted her pace as I sped up. Zoe trotted beside me, grinning. We rounded the muddy edge of the lagoon then proceeded down the Causeway into the mossy, permanent shade of Stanley Park's giant cedars.

It was cool in there. Cold, almost. Quiet too. The soft, fabric-like bark of the cedars soaked up sound like a sponge, and in the silence my paranoid thoughts were magnified to operatic levels.

Tanya held Zoe's hand tight as we threaded our way between abandoned cars, parked bumper to bumper across all three lanes. For five minutes we walked deeper and deeper into the park, the absolute silence occasionally given a hairline fracture by the fading cries of English Bay seagulls.

And then I saw them.

To our left, a pair of men were moving through the bush on a bike trail that paralleled the Causeway. An odd couple—one lanky and fair, the other squat and dark. The tall one was a skater punk, outfitted with a jabbering T-shirt and long, long black shorts tricked out with chains. The shorter one looked like an accountant. Slacks and loafers—a kind of autistic stab at *Mad Men*-style trendiness. Ironic, of course, given that he was now literally insane. But none of the tribal signals indicated by the pair's clothing mattered, really; they were united by filth, wild eyes, and perfectly matching expressions of intense concentration. They were hunting.

But hunting what? The park's fat, tourist-fed squirrels? I squinted further ahead, deeper into the woods and saw, toddling obliviously along, their real quarry.

A pair of Sleeper children.

Two small boys, hand in hand, were trundling down the path, a hundred or so feet ahead of their pursuers. You'd have thought they were off to get an ice cream cone from the concession stand at Lumberman's Arch. But you'd have thought wrong.

Behind them, the Mad Man shushed the Skater, bade him wait, and increased his own pace.

Grabbing Tanya's arm and pointing at them, I pantomimed instructions that she and Zoe should hide themselves behind a nearby SUV and wait for me. Then, bar in hand, I set off in pursuit.

My stomach churned, but I knew what I had to do. Either I would take out the pursuers or they would take out the children. A simple either/or choice. Or, rather, no choice. And when I realized I had no choice, a weight lifted from my shoulders. It was so odd to realize that choice had been a burden I'd been lugging around all my life—and that choice had only really existed because, until now, nothing particularly important had been at stake.

Ahead of me, the Skater slowed and stopped, his battery running low. Sneaking up behind him was no big deal, and neither, as it turned out, was lifting my dumbbell and bringing it down on his head. The bar sank into his skull, black blood welling up around the wound, and the skater toppled to the ground. Human skulls as easy to smash as watermelons? I'd say that was about right. What did I feel at that moment? I don't want to understate or overstate the case, but *not that much*. The death, my act of murder, felt TV-remote; the reality of those two little boys overrode any squeamishness or pity I might have been inclined to feel.

And decisiveness was a pretty empowering feeling.

Later that night I'd reflect and feel nauseous at what I'd done, but even then—and even now when the memory occasionally bloats up and floats back to the surface of my mind—animal horror is tinged by pride that I had *acted*, had saved two lives. But WWJD? What would Jesus have done in my position? My money would be on the barbell.

The Mad Man hadn't heard a thing: he was too far ahead, too intent on his task. I heaved the dripping bar back over my shoulder and carried on, pure and cold in my purpose, like I was made of iron myself. The weapon wasn't an extension of me, as cliché would have it, but rather I was an extension of the weapon.

The trail ahead was a minefield of twigs and branches, dangerous terrain for someone hoping to make a sneak attack. As I drew closer to the Mad Man, I saw that he did indeed have a knife—a long, curved kitchen blade. I began to hurry, but before I could reach him, he spun around. To my surprise, his face wasn't hostile. It was conspiratorial.

Hushing me, he pointed over his shoulder at the strolling boys and whispered, 'Demons!' like I'd understand and immediately get with the program.

I hoisted my bar again. He looked up, saw his partner's blood and brains spackled on it, then fell to his knees and began to whimper.

'Oh God, Oh dear God, Holy Shit, what have I done?' he cried, and began to alternate sobs and oaths.

Up ahead, the boys heard his voice, let go of each other's hands and bounded like startled rabbits. Then they ducked into the first available gap in the underbrush and vanished. I turned my attention back to the Mad Man, who was still burbling out chains of prayer.

'Oh God, oh God, oh God.'

I'd programmed myself for a second kill, but the sight of easy prey on its knees, to all appearances overflowing with sincere remorse, stopped me in my tracks.

'What were you doing?'

He buried his face in his hands. His hands then spoke.

'If you catch one and drink its blood, you get to sleep. They have the Sleepy Time blood. Like red chamomile tea. Have you seen their *eyes*? They're crammed full of zeds. The fucking park's swarming with them. Fuck fuck fuck fuck fuck…'

He was drifting from grief toward frustration and rage. I reached down, snatched the knife out of his hand, and hurled it as far as I could into the bush.

'Get a grip,' I hissed. 'They're not demons. They're just little kids.'

He rattled his head back and forth. 'How do you know? You don't know. Every time I pass by the fucking lagoon I see them peeking out through the bushes at me. And they're always giggling. Why are they laughing at us when we're fucking dying?'

'They aren't hurting anyone. They were just two little kids walking through the park.'

He released his face from his hands and fixed his eyes on mine.

'Not hurting anyone? They hurt me! They hurt my fucking retinas! They burn a hole through my shitting brains. Every thought I have, there's one of those kids burned through the middle of it. Not hurting anyone? Fuck you. Know what I saw yesterday over on Denman Street?

I waited.

'A kid's arm, man. In the middle of the street. Just an arm. And other little kids walking around with blood and shit all over themselves. Our kids, real kids. Not Demons. So what's not demonic about *them,* out here, looking like everything's fucking copacetic? Do *you* know what's in their blood?'

Tanya was watching us. The Mad Man saw her too.

'Just get out of here,' I told him. 'And don't follow us. Go back downtown.'

I hated the sound and sense of all the words available to me, a nauseous swirl of chimp thoughts and grunted syllables. It had felt much better to simply hoist the bar and let it drop.

I turned away, but he stopped me with a hand around my ankle.

'Do me a favour before you go.'

I pulled away and looked at him. He was smiling up at me, pine needles the colour of dried blood sticking to his left cheek.

'What?'

'Kill me, man. It won't get better. Right? This isn't going to stop. And I won't stop hunting. You know I won't. As soon as you're gone, I'll be looking for another kid. So do it. Stop me. I'll turn around so you don't have to look in my eyes.'

He shuffled around on his knees until he was facing away from me, palms flat on the ground, head raised high. Like Tanya ready for a sleepy-bye fuck.

I looked back at Tanya, who was watching me intently, something glinting in her eyes. I couldn't see Zoe.

'I can't,' I said after a moment. 'I can't do it.'

Not in cold blood, anyway. If he'd made a move in my direction, I'd have done it in a heartbeat, but he didn't move. So I walked away.

By the time I got back to Tanya and Zoe, the Mad Man was up on his feet again.

'Big mistake, fucker!' he screamed. 'Big fucking mistake. I'm your fucking shadow now, you hear me?! When you're asleep, I'm going to take *you* out and drink *your* blood, you sleeping motherfucker! I saw that fucking mascara all over your face! And when I've done you, I'll take care of your fucking traitor bitch girlfriend! And then your little bitch demon!'

Tanya glared at me with naked scorn. Zoe sat at her ankles, scratching idly at the asphalt with a stick.

'Why didn't you do it, Paul? What? You were man enough to kill the first one when his back was turned, but you didn't have the guts to take out the second one even though he was begging for it. What if he comes after Zoe? Man up, Paul. This isn't a joke. This isn't one of your stupid books.'

She was wrong about that, of course.

The Mad Man was still there, listening.

'You know what? I'm so fucking glad you didn't kill me, dude! I just got confused for a second, that's all. I'll be seeing you soon. I'll remember you. You better remember me!'

Then he turned and started walking back toward the city, whistling and swinging his arms. I watched for a while to see if he would try to turn around and follow us. But he didn't, and soon enough he disappeared around a bend in the Causeway. We pressed on.

Five more minutes' walking brought us within sight of Lion's Gate Bridge. Viewed from the woods, the bridge is a spectacular sight. Framed by imperial forest it arches up into the sky like a man-made rainbow. A breeze is always blowing across Coal Harbour and that wind, though invisible, is somehow a part of the picture: the bridge so still, but with invisible motion rippling across it. And on the mountains behind the bridge, the twin peaks of the lions themselves: they were there before we came to North America and stuck a name on them—and they'll be there long after we're gone.

The line of abandoned cars extended from where we stood all the way up to the crest of the bridge where a clash of colours caught my eye. Fabric flapped and snapped. Tiny figures moved to and fro as though on the deck of a giant, impossible ship.

'What the hell is that?' I asked. Rhetorically. All my questions were rhetorical now, I realized, given that Zoe wouldn't answer and Tanya saw me as either a useless fool or a dangerous one.

'I wouldn't go up there if I were you, Paul,' a familiar voice behind me answered.

Charles. My shoulders slumped while Tanya froze in her footsteps beside me.

'There's an unfriendly city being built up there by some pretty uncompaniable people, Paul. Not like us. They aren't people of the book.'

I turned around. Charles wasn't alone. Arrayed behind him were about two dozen of his people, a strange and terrible crew. They'd been rich, they'd been poor. They'd been young and old, but now they were all the same in their greasiness and their gritty, gummy eyes, all stuck on me.

There was more than safety in Charles' numbers: there was consensus, there was culture, there was reality. Surrounded by a wasteland of isolates, Charles bore the gift of order. When Charles moved, his people moved. When he stood still, they did the same.

'Are you ready to come home, Paul? Done sightseeing?'

Tanya was staring at Charles, dumbfounded. He accepted her stare with royal bemusement.

'Hey, Tanya? How's it hanging?'

'I'm good. Good.'

She shocked me with the timidity of her reply. I'd expected withering scorn but heard…acceptance.

Charles nodded.

'I just wanted to say something to you, Tanya. I know we parted on bad terms last week, but no hard feelings? It's a new day, so let's make a fresh start.'

Tanya made a half nod, which is to say her chin sank down to her chest and stayed there. I considered our options, but there was no way to escape. We'd be going back downtown.

'Let's get going,' Charles said, pointing at the bridge. A handful of tiny figures were moving down the bridge's arc toward us.

Quickly, then, we began to retrace our footsteps down the Causeway. And as we walked, Charles spoke to Tanya of Nod while I gripped Zoe's hand and bit my lip.

Charles chattered away to Tanya like a nervous sophomore trying to impress a cheerleader.

'All the days before were false starts, rehearsals for the Eternal Day. What we called Time was just the tally of those false starts. Sun up, sun down. Tick, tick, tick. Past, present, future. Plod, plod, plod. And by sleeping, we'd get amnesia each day because we weren't ready for life. Put it all down to rehearsal, to not being ready. And now the rehearsal is over and we're awake and given this world to do something with.'

Tanya listened without comment, but also without scorn. Charles' crew were listening to the story too. They nodded to one another and smacked their lips dryly in a manner that indicated they'd heard this non-bedtime story before.

'But it's so scary.'

Said Tanya.

Charles nodded.

'Yes, scary. We're going through a big change. Imagine how you must have felt when you were a newborn baby, leaving the womb and being forced, squeezed, out into the light and the world. Hunger and anger. Loss and gain. All of that. Imagine how it must have felt. But you got over it, right? You dealt with it.'

'I guess so.' She was staring vacantly into the distance, but I could tell she was listening.

'Well, this is the same thing, only it's being done to our minds, not our bodies. Scary, scary, scary. And some people can't handle being Awake. And that's okay. They run off and hide in sleep, which is really the same as saying they want to die. They don't want to *be*. They crave *oblivion*. And that's death.'

That brought her back to earth. Tanya glared at me and Zoe.

'They can always die. We can help them die if that's what they really want. Or we can help them to live.'

'But if this is so wonderful, why am I so ugly?' Tanya whispered, fingering her lank hair with quivering fingers, her face corpse-pale beneath its dead weight.

'Ugly is as ugly does,' Charles replied, almost leaping on

her question. He appeared to have an answer for everything. 'The little Sleeper Demons in the woods aren't pretty. They're a mockery. Little shiny plastic toys. They look like people but they're not!' He softened his tone. 'Pretty is as pretty does.'

'Tell us about the Sleepers!' cried a voice from the crowd, a gaunt man with a skull grin. 'I want to hear more about the Sleepers!'

Charles spoke more loudly. 'The Sleepers are the failures! Throwbacks! Nodgod didn't see fit to bring them along on the journey into the Eternal Now. Like he left behind the apes when he brought man up!'

Here Charles' minions laughed as though on cue. Some of them began grunting and hopping.

'They can't stand in the light or the night of Eternal Day.'

Laughter.

'They run and hide their sleepyheads when the sun falls down.'

Jeers.

'They'll keep hiding in Oblivion and then they'll just fade and die. Like flowers planted among the spiders in a cave. By a madman.'

'But the TV said we're the ones who're going to die...' the questioner's voice trailed off and there was silence. All eyes fixed on Charles as he bowed his head, striving to master a thought or a feeling, or maybe to become a statue. When he spoke, his gaze flickered past everyone in regular rotation.

'Don't talk to me about time. Haven't you got ears? There are no days, there is no 'month'. This isn't today and it isn't yesterday or the future either. You won't die in 'a month' because there is no month. Eternity is right now. And why has Nodgod given us this Eternal Day?'

'To fill it with our works,' came the reply from a dozen pairs of dry lips. 'To build a new city.'

'And will we rest?'

'Never.'

'And are there demons in the woods and Rawhead Bloody-Bones strolling around the streets with our teeth rattling in their pockets?'

'Yes.'

'And who is the Admiral of the Blue?'

'He who will rebuild a city that will last forever in one Eternal Day.'

Zoe was standing beside me, staring expressionlessly up at Charles. I reached down and took her hand, but she pulled it away. Then Charles turned to me and did something strange.

He winked.

And then something even more strange.

The sky above the cedars flashed white and our shadows, which had lain placidly behind us, were scalded into the asphalt. Blinded, I pulled Zoe toward me and we fell flat on the ground.

Somewhere in time and space I heard a voice thick with hysterical revelation: Charles'.

'The Brazen Head! The Brazen Head has spoken!!'

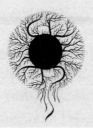

DAY 8
WAKING A WITCH

If a 'witch' was obdurate, the most effectual way of obtaining a confession was by 'waking' her. For this purpose an iron bridle or hoop was bound across her face with four prongs thrust into her mouth. The bridle was fastened to a wall in such a way as the 'witch' was unable to lie down, while men were constantly by to keep her awake.

'There's someone here you need to meet,' Charles whispered, his dumpster breath coiling into my ear.

I opened my watering eyes, my single mandated hour of sleep now over. This regimen was making my eyes twitch, and I occasionally saw electric flickers of movement in the periphery of my vision—coming attractions, I supposed, for the visions of Nod the Awakened were seeing all around them. An hour wasn't long enough to allow me the Dream, and its absence left me sullen and resentful. And yet, my meagre ration of sleep had to have been a bounty compared to the absolute zero that Tanya and everyone else around me was subsisting on. I couldn't imagine and still can't. All I think of when I try to imagine absolute sleeplessness is a single day that never ends—a good working definition of Hell. Hell is time, isn't that obvious? Take your greatest pleasure or your greatest fantasy and let it come continuously true—for a day, a week, a year, a decade. And that's hell.

Behind Charles' blue-clad form, gritty, Tang-coloured light swam through the classroom window. Seattle dust.

Ever since we'd arrived back from Stanley Park, my mind kept compulsively returning to the awful light that had thrown us down on our faces. The flash had only lasted a fraction of a second but had left us temporarily blind. We lay on the Causeway with our arms over our heads long after the light died away, terrified it would happen again. All around me a chorus of panting and retching, and the scratching of fabric on asphalt. Voices whimpered Charles' name, and when he answered them, I could hear aftershocks rippling through his Admiral Voice. As for me, the insides of my eyelids were scarred with bright, pale patches of light.

It wasn't until we picked ourselves up and looked across the park toward the clear blue skies south of us that we realized what had actually happened.

There, in the sky across English Bay and above Point Grey, stood a mushroom cloud, still and imperious, stretching from the horizon to the upper limits of the atmosphere, where it squashed up against outer space. We could just see the cloud's thick, cottony stem, obscured by distance and horizon, but its massive head was fully visible.

Someone had hit Seattle, two hundred-odd kilometres to the south, with a nuclear warhead. For the first time since this whole thing had begun, tears came into my eyes. Tears for whom? For myself? For Tanya? For a few million dead Americans? To be honest, at that moment I was more inclined to envy the dead than to mourn them. And even if I'd wanted to mourn, four or five million were too many to shed tears over. Tears are more personal than that. We don't read a news story about twenty thousand dead in an earthquake and *weep*. At best, we sigh and tell the wife. More often, we shrug and go check our Facebook messages.

Really, I don't know why I cried. Maybe I wept for the sake of *scale* as I imagined us all as viewed from a cosmic distance, so tiny and insignificant. From space, even that gigantic cloud would be nothing more than a tiny pimple on Earth's fat, round face. I remembered my hypothetical asteroid, the one that might wipe out the planet while we slept. Now it had happened, to Seattle, and who was to say but that there might be a sister missile to the one that hit Vancouver's sister city fizzing our way across the Pacific right now?

All our sci-fi nightmares were coming true. And then a thought hit me: *everything we can imagine is possible*. Everything. All my life I, along with most of the rest of the world, had been subjected to an endless loop of cultural snuff porn: annihilation by nuke, war, economic catastrophe, and/or zombie attack. But I'd never taken it seriously. Maybe, by crying, I was mourning an innocence that, a week ago, I'd have indignantly denied I possessed.

In the end, though, I think I wept because I just didn't understand it. Any of it. And when my tears eventually stopped flowing, did it mean that I'd understood? Or was it that my brain or soul was simply too small to hold such massive grief for more than a few moments? Had grief just paused near me for a moment, shrugged and moved on?

'Paul?' Charles was still crouched beside me, reeking and creaking as he leaned in much too close, 'Time to get to work.'

I stood quickly, trying to avoid proximity. Zoe was still asleep in her nest of blankets beneath the teacher's desk, choke-holding the stuffed grizzly. Tanya had told Zoe its name was Ralph or something, but a name had no way of sticking to our silent ward and slid off onto the floor before being kicked into a thoughtless corner. The namelessness of Noddish bears. That said, Zoe seemed to have formed a real attachment to the creature. It was hard to imagine Zoe needing anything, but there you were: everywhere she went, the bear went too.

Charles and I had cut a deal when we'd arrived at the school: a room with a lockable door for the three of us. A safe place to hide the dangerous shame of mine and Zoe's sleeping from Charles' acolytes.

But where was Tanya?

'She's working,' Charles said, somehow able to read my thoughts.

'Working?'

'We keep busy. Nice and safe and snug and working hard. Tomorrow Never Comes. Right? But why am I telling you?' He actually paused and smacked his forehead with the palm of his hand. 'It's in your book! What does procrastination mean, Paul? It means waiting for tomorrow. There's no time like today. Ha! There's no time BUT today. Life must flow in unbroken lines...'

Charles was chanting these words, mostly to himself. He had been pretty displaced in the old world, but he fit into 'Nod' better than anybody else I'd met so far. His words didn't flow in 'unbroken lines' of logic, but they did flow steadily, and when they encountered a logical obstacle, they just flowed right around it. There was a crooked man, who walked a crooked mile. And here were Tanya, Zoe, and I, deep inside his crooked house.

'What sort of work is she doing?'

'This. That. This and that. This, that, and the other. Come with me, and I'll show you.' He saw me look toward Zoe, the back of whose tousled head was just visible from where we stood and sneered. 'Don't worry, Paul. No one will fuck with the little demon while you're gone.'

When Charles called Zoe a demon that first time, I took it as irony, just like when he'd winked at me after addressing his massed masses the day before. Charles occupied a funny place in Nod, as far as I could see. I'm pretty sure he knew the new world order he was trying to orchestrate was 'made up'—after all, he was making it up himself—and that the children in the park weren't literally demons. On one level. On another level, he didn't have a clue. I found myself thinking of Moses coming down from the mountain carrying stone tablets and raving about some burning bush, of Jesus in his lonesome desert, checkmating the devil and emerging with a mission. Were these fantastical revelations simply fibs that turned into delusions that turned into accepted truths centuries later? Consider Joseph Smith, Jr, the founder of Mormonism only a century and a half ago. He'd been a small time salesman and huckster; then one day he claimed that an angel had dictated a new book of the Bible to him. And within no time whatsoever his spiel was granted that special hands-over-ears status we accord religion. Smith tended to look crazier than Jesus or Moses to many, but that might be because he was simply the most recent of the last three millennia's worth of prophets. They were just newer. Or consider L. Ron Hubbard and Scientology. Nothing particularly wacky about his visions of telepathic aliens compared to those of his predecessors. Scientology would fit Nod like a leather glove.

And here, next in line, stood Charles, thinking up a storm. He was taking pages from my poor, unfinished manuscript, yanking out words, and using them to name things. It was as though he'd been Cain, wandering the earth for millennia before finally finding his way back to a broken and abandoned Garden of Eden, where everything had been uprooted and thrown about by a petulant God. And now Cain was tidying up the mess, completing the naming process that had been abandoned by his disgraced father, Adam.

Me.

Suddenly I wanted nothing more than to crawl into a closet, barricade myself there, and dream my Dream forever. How long since this drawn-out ending had begun? Eight days? Nine? I'd already lost count. If the Brazen Heads were right, there was only another two weeks until the bodies of the Awakened followed their minds into the abyss. How much more madness would froth up before it was over? Surely there was only so crazy a person could become and still be able to eat, drink, and stand upright. Certain logical patterns of organization pertaining to movement and vision had to be maintained. Or so I hoped.

'Come with me,' Charles snapped. I was seeing a pattern. He was servile when we were around his people but bossy as hell when we were alone.

I locked the classroom using the key Charles had solemnly handed me the night before, as though I was too stupid to know it had twin upon twin. We made our way down the locker-lined hallway to a door at the far end.

A half dozen or so of Charles' followers were milling about, all engaged in some sort of clockwork task or another. One woman, her face obscured by curds of matted hair, stood hunchbacked in a doorway, murmuring into a dead cell phone cupped in her hands. Occasionally, she would stab at the keys of its text pad.

Charles snorted. 'She's talking to the dead. On her dead cell phone. Let the dead message the dead.'

Next to her an enormously fat man, a stub of a broom in his hands, was endlessly sweeping the same patch of floor. The linoleum beneath his broom was wearing thin. A patch of liquid pooled at his feet. Piss. I held my breath.

'A—Admiral…' he said as we passed.

'Yes?'

'What did Nodgod tell you yesterday in the park?'

'Didn't you hear His oration?' Charles asked, apparently disgusted.

'I just fell down. I was too scared.' The fat man shook his head and his jowls flapped. There's a point of obesity where, like it or not, whatever your other personal achievements or qualities, all you are is 'the fat man' or 'the fat lady'. The world is a gawking four-year-old.

'Soon enough I'll share with you all what Nodgod revealed to me.'

The fat man was weeping. 'Thank you, Admiral.'

I'd like to describe Charles' followers in more detail, but there was a lank and greasy sameness to them that makes it difficult. Weight, age, and gender were about all that differentiated them—and guessing gender was starting to be a crap shoot. Perhaps the wellspring of their uniformity lay in the identical expressions on their grey faces. They were catatonic patients in a mental ward who might suddenly fly into superhuman rages for no reason. Desks might fly. Dolls might dismember. Dull and dangerous, they needed to be medicated, but the pharmacies were empty.

One thing they all had in common was a task. Each of them was doing something. Or, rather, each of them was doing anything— it didn't seem to matter what. Busy work. One old man was folding newspaper pages into tiny squares and stacking them neatly on a table. A teen-aged girl beside him was busily cutting another sheet of newspaper into confetti, slowly, laboriously.

'We aren't pokes, but we do poke about,' Charles said, noticing my curiosity. 'And if we don't, we'll get such a poke.'

He wanted to see if his Nod-erudition was impressing me. The word 'poke' has several meanings. First, 'a lazy person', second, to busy oneself without definite object'.

'I read this,' he held up my manuscript, 'almost all the time. What strikes me about the word 'poke' is how it has two completely opposite meanings. Think of the power!'

'Power?'

'We can rename. If we need to we can even change the meaning of words. Or make up new ones and make them mean what we want. And that's how we'll do it.'

'Do what?'

'My eyes are changing, Paul! I see new things—and I can name them with your words. When Nodgod spoke yesterday, the meaning of it all just about swallowed me whole! He's wiping the slate clean, giving us sanction to start over! You must be so fucking thrilled, Paul! Most writers just hope to get a few people to read their stuff, but your book is going to create a whole new world. You're a prophet.'

'Not me. This is your game, not mine.'

Charles spun toward me so quickly I thought he might fall over. As it was, he staggered.

'No! This didn't come from me! I'm the messenger, but you're the vessel! Just be sure you're a worthy vessel. Word to the wise.'

We had now arrived at the door at the far end of the hall. A sinewy Asian man whose muscular arms and chest were covered in tattoos stood in front of it. When Charles opened the door, he shuffled silently to one side, and after we entered, I heard him shuffle back into position.

A long and skinny room, a book room. Two windows at

the far end in the dusky distance. Charles led me between the shelves of books, thirty or so copies of each title, most of them, judging by the crappiness of their designs, relics of the eighties or nineties. Halloween orange spines. Futuristic fonts on taped-up covers.

Then another door at the back.

He paused, hand on the doorknob, suddenly solicitous.

'There's somebody in here that you really need to meet, Paul.'

He went in, and I followed. To our right an old woman shrouded in rags crouched on the floor, cradling a metal shish kebab skewer in both hands. She looked up at me and tittered. Directly across from her, slumped against the far wall, was a man in his early twenties. He looked up. Despite the haggard, exhausted look on his face, I could tell right away that he was a fellow Sleeper. One end of a bike chain was locked around his throat; the other was attached to a thick metal pipe that ran from the floor to the ceiling.

He wore khaki shorts and a torn and stained T-shirt with Captain America on the front. Someone who had, until recently, appreciated kitsch. Now his T-shirt looked terribly sad, like a Spice Girls T-shirt from the 1990s that you might see on a hungry African kid in a charity appeal. We'd put so much stock in T-shirts. Personal flags replacing, perhaps, national ones in an age of ascendant ego. But here in Nod, the single citizen nation state of Captain America had been overrun, its flag torn down and trampled.

Captain America's arms were covered in small cuts and oozing welts that showed no signs of healing. It wasn't hard to figure out where they had come from. Or why they'd been inflicted. Meanwhile, Skewer Woman lovingly polished her weapon.

Charles' voice took on a wheedling tone as he tried to forestall my objections.

'Therapy, Paul. Salvation. But not punishment. Not cruelty.'

Skewer Lady nodded in confirmation.

'He's been good. Pretty good.' She made a tentative stab in the direction of her prisoner. 'Scissors to grind. Scissors to grind.'

'Who are you?' the prisoner stared at me, agog. 'You're not one of them.'

'I know it's ugly, surface ugly, Paul, but try to see this as triage in a war zone. Think of it as love. There's Truth all around him, but he can't *be* it so long as he keeps drifting off into Oblivion. Like a dog, like a fucking booze hound running for the bottle. He keeps turning away from the sun. So he gets burned. What's a sun to do?'

'He keeps hiding his eyes,' the old woman joined in, nodding and weaving, 'but the sun is always shining. He falls flat on his face and tries to worship the night. I've seen him!'

She lunged at him, but Charles kicked her arm away. She pulled back into herself, whimpering.

'Only if he tries to sleep, Judy. You know better than that.'

Judy. It seemed impossible that her name was Judy.

Muttering, she settled back down into her corner.

'Did they get you too?' Captain America asked me, his face contorted as he tried to paste me into his world. 'Fuck. No, that's not it. You're with them! Why aren't you tied up? Why don't you run?! Oh, God!'

'Shut up,' Charles said casually, and the prisoner jerked just as if someone had yanked hard on his chain. 'No one wants to hear what you have to say. 'Scornful dogs will eat dirty puddings'. You'll see things differently in a day or two when you wake up. And then you'll thank us.'

Charles addressed me. 'This is sin, Paul. You should hear him babble about the dream he was having when we found him…'

'His precious dream!' Judy spat. 'His darling dream world filled with golden light!'

Back out in the book room, Charles grabbed my arm. 'Do you see now?'

Behind the closed door, Captain America was screaming.

I was shaking. 'See what?'

'We're the children of Cain, Paul. We've wandered through the day and the night for thousands of years. It's been our punishment. But now it's ending. We're waking up from our dream and seeing what Nodgod wants us to see! That one,' Charles sneered back over his shoulder, 'is offensive to the Unsleeping Lord who gave us this day! And you. You, you, you. You see. You wrote the book that describes it all. But you still sleep and you pal around with demons. And I can't quite figure it out…'

Charles fell silent and began to pace. I waited as he wandered up and down the aisles, his fingers trailing, as I imagined, along the spines of high school classics: *The Chrysalids* and *Animal Farm*. *Lord of the Flies*. *1984*. Apocalypse and dystopia. Despairing visions. Every high school had taught these books. Every teen had been injected with them. What had possessed us?

Charles' footsteps stopped in the next aisle.

'Do you know your Bible, Paul? I know mine. Do you know about Moses?'

I did, and my mouth went dry.

'Moses, Paul, guided the Chosen People to the Promised Land but God did not allow him to enter.' A pause. 'Now, why was that?'

'I don't know.'

Charles walked back to the aisle where I stood.

'I don't know either, Paul, but I'm starting to have thoughts.'

He stared at me without blinking, like he was trying to burn away some obscuring film that concealed me.

'What thoughts, Ch—Admiral?'

A smile twitched across his face.

'So much in names, so much in what we say and don't say. So much in what we almost say. So much in what we never think to say. Or hide away. Maybe God had a little bitsy problem with Moses. Can you guess what sort of problem?'

'No, I can't.'

Closer. 'Maybe God thought Moses was a little too arrogant, doing God's work for him.' Closer. 'Maybe Moses got himself and God mixed up.' Far too close. 'Maybe Moses thought he *was* God.'

Then the clouds blew away and Charles was grinning.

'Or maybe not. Who knows! Time's a tattletale, Paul. It'll spill all the beans eventually. And here in Nod, there's lots and lots of time. All will be revealed.'

I sensed an opening in his good humour. 'Where's Tanya?'

'Tanya? She's working. I already told you that.'

'No. I mean, I'd like to go talk to her.'

He came back around into my aisle, shrugging. 'Go for it. She's wiping down some chalkboards. Top floor. First door on the south side.'

I turned to go.

'But what about *your* work, Paul?'

'What work?'

'You've got a speech to give tomorrow morning. Remember? Right now my people are out on the streets, spreading the word. There are about fifty of us now, but I need a thousand.'

'A thousand?'

He ignored me even as he answered. 'A thousand's the number for a Rabbit Hunt.'

Rabbit hunt? The term didn't ring any bells, didn't come from my manuscript.

'What's a—?'

'Go see to your Tanya, Paul. Go check on your little pet demon, too—but keep it locked up. If anyone with open eyes sees it, it might get squashed. Anyone with open eyes would think the thing had just crawled out of Demon Park.'

Demon Park. I didn't even have to stop to think what that meant. The new words were falling into place with shocking ease.

When I found Tanya, it was somehow no surprise to see her scrubbing intently at a small patch of chalk-free blackboard. Sweat dimpled her forehead and she was working her jaw, grinding her teeth. I came up behind and put my hands gently on her shoulders.

She turned and clawed at me until I backed away. Then she stood still, head down, face covered by lank hair, as she heaved bales of breath in and out of her chest, a striped red and blue eraser still clutched in her trembling right hand.

'Medusa?' I said gently.

'Don't call me that! Medusa was a monster. Do you think I'm a monster?'

Then she looked up, and I saw a monster.

About as much of my Tanya remained in the face that now seethed at me as remains in a photo album from which all the prints have been torn and shredded; nothing there but yellowish outlines where pretty pictures had once lain. A plundered past— nothing but teases for my poor, pathetic memory. Tanya was gone.

In the sun-soaked classroom her dear, dear face, resembled a shrunken head in a natural history museum. Ancient and unknowably foreign, lopped off and dried mid-scream. Denied a decent burial. I could go on. I do go on.

Back to her question. Did I think she was a monster? Did I think that eight days had undone an entire life, undone two intertwined lives? That was the burning question and it was a real bonfire, the burning bush of a question I'm still here trying to face, still trying to answer.

So back to her question.

'No. You're not a monster.'

Where just a couple of days earlier, love had been Omission, now it was a bald-faced lie. Love a lie. But a real lie, a *true* lie. 'Charles doesn't think I'm a monster.'

'Charles? Since when do you care what Charles thinks?'

She squinted, trying to fix me in her glare. 'I was wrong about him.'

There was no point in arguing. I was sure that, to Tanya, Charles did make sense.

Casually. 'We should talk, Paul.'

'About what?'

'A lot of things. About bedtime arrangements. About demons. About putting makeup on sleepy-bye eyes.'

I could see that she wanted to turn back to her chalkboard, that she was forcing herself to keep facing me as though I was the monster, impossible to look upon. Emotions heaved and shuddered within me, rising and falling but unable to escape the gravitational field of my body. I was seasick with feeling as grey sea serpents of horror and mourning roiled in my gut. That was my real welcome to Nod, I think. Until that moment, part of the old world had been alive in me in the form of hope. But now that votive candle had been snuffed, and I was a wisp of climbing smoke.

'You won't miss me while you're snoozing, Paul.' She stretched her head forwards and upwards as she examined my jaw line from below. 'But you look so sad! Lost something precious? I can comfort you if you like. How about I share some juicy secrets with you? It might take a little of the sting away.'

She began to slap the eraser into her free palm, causing clouds of chalk dust to rise and whiten her. Hard and harder.

'I would have left you.'

I bit my lip.

'I can see it in your eyes! Ha! You know it too!'

I said nothing, tried not to think.

'It wasn't enough, what we had. You know that. You know you weren't offering me enough. You fucking idiot. No friends, no life. Your stupid books and your stupid fucking sour attitude! There was nothing there to make a life from. One more fucking sushi night with us alone in that apartment might have done me in! You hate people. You wanted me to hate people, and if I'd stayed with you that's what would have happened. You know what? I bet you're glad that this happened. I bet you think we all deserved it. That's why you wrote that book of yours.'

She paused to gather her ammunition and shot me a wild look that didn't contain an ounce of regret.

'Well, guess what? Fuck Sushi Fridays. You remember another little ritual? My girls' nights out? With Tori Strawberry? Well, they weren't just girls' nights out, not sometimes. You'd sit there at home, too good to go out and party. But we partied. Lots of stiff, fat cocks. So fucking easy to find. You men are so fucking easy! They say girls are easy, but it's fucking boys and their fucking cocks! Smile at them and—boing—they're out and rubbing against you. You never had me, not really, Paul.' She stopped and watched me. 'Why so glum, chum? There's nothing to cry about.'

This was no news. The evening when she told me she'd been abused by an uncle, I'd held her and felt special, like we shared a burden. And other things she hadn't told me but which I'd been able to discern in her eyes when she drank hard liquor. This was no news.

She leaned still further forward and turned her head sideways, neck cricking.

'Don't be such a baby, Paul. Anything you want to say? Any questions? I've got work to do. Charles says that idle hands… but you know all those old sayings, don't you, Mr. Prophet.'

I turned and fumbled my way to the door. At the last moment, though, she called me back.

'Paul. Look at me, Paul.'

Her voice had changed. I turned and looked at her. For a strobe-lit second, she was herself again.

'It isn't true. I didn't do anything bad. I love you, Paul. Always remember that, no matter what I say or what you see me do. This is true, right now. The rest is all lies. Darling.'

Then she sniggered, spat at my feet, and turned back to her work.

For hours after that, I was as fragile as the shell of a battery egg. If I'd touched anything, I'd have shattered and pale yellow soul-yolk would have slithered out of me and puddled on the floor. I stayed locked in what was now mine and Zoe's classroom, struggling to hold a face together for the child's benefit, not that she seemed to require such support. When Charles would call through the door for me, I'd answer 'soon' to whatever it was he was saying and hold my breath until he left. Mostly, though, I just waited for the pain to kill me.

But it didn't. I just endured. And through enduring, I learned suffering's dirty little secret: the sufferer is always bigger than the pain. You roll around on the floor like a baby. You vomit up tears. You shit your thoughts into a plastic bag and try to asphyxiate them. I did all that. And still existence persisted. From the ceaselessly beckoning no-time of my Dream to an empty classroom where time burned endlessly like a torture cell light bulb: through it all, pain remained something inside me— remained, therefore, something ultimately smaller than me.

Visions stabbed at me with their kebab skewers. Tanya in a hotel room. Tanya in a bar. Laughing, dancing, sucking, moaning. An animal she—and an animal me, spasmodically imagining it all. Had she been telling the truth? Had she been lying? I still have no idea. Both possibilities seemed to carry equal weight.

Eventually I realized that someone was watching me. Zoe.

The bear peeked out from behind her crossed arms—four eyes fixed on mine. And somehow eyes brought me back from wherever I'd been. And as I returned, a matryoshka doll of nested feelings opened up before me: mine for Tanya; Tanya's for Zoe; Zoe's for the bear.

Tanya was gone, the Dream lay ahead, and in between them lay the necessity of some sort of safe haven for a child in this mad world.

By midnight I knew what I had to do. I emerged to face Charles, looking better in his eyes by virtue of looking so bad, and we walked the candle-lit halls and discussed what I was going to say the next morning. Occasionally, screams and moans drifted in from the Book Room. And just like I'd ignored the more unsavoury parts of the news a week ago, I tried my best to ignore them. For the moment.

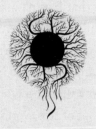

DAY 9
PANJANDRUM

*A village boss, who imagines himself the
'Magnus Apollo' of his neighbours.*

Dear Diary, So what's the deal with all this dear diarizing?

In order to write or, more precisely, to be sane and write, one needs either an audience or at least some idea of an audience; there's a fine line between 'writing' and babbling to oneself. You can't just write to no one—even if no one ends up reading what you've written. And with the world about to end and everyone I've ever known either dead or done for, that's a problematic caveat as I sit here scribbling away on this pad of yellow paper. I tell myself writing helps keep me awake, keeps me from drifting off permanently into the golden light, but that's not really the whole truth.

So who *are* you, invisible reader? You're not one of the

Awakened, and I don't think you're the kids in the park, either. Neither of those groups strike me as particularly bookish. Are you one of my fellow Sleeper adults? But surely I'm not spilling any beans here that haven't already been pelted down on their heads by the million. They've *had* the dream. They've *lost* everything and everyone. They don't *need* this little memoir. Besides, they won't be hanging around Nod much longer either: their dreams will swallow them up whole about the same time the Awakened pass on out of this world. So who are you?

Maybe you're alien archaeologists and you've discovered this yellow tablet a thousand years from now. Maybe you're a diary-snooping God. But then again, maybe you're the truth, and you just need some figuring out.

Shortly before dawn, Charles's red-veined hands jerked me from my Dream and back into Time. Time for our chat with the loping, oozing citizenry of Nod. Time for my debut.

While I gnawed at a rancid bagel that tasted for all the world just like a rancid bagel (one retrieved from a dumpster and given a good polish by a sticky shirt sleeve), Charles fussed about *where* the speech was going to happen.

'We could have it in the gym, but there are only fifty of us and it might look empty. We could have it outside, but who knows what could happen out there.'

His school marm-ish anxieties were almost endearing. You could tell he wanted to ask my opinion but was worried I'd mock him. In the end he decided we would speak on the front steps of the school. There, we'd be within earshot of the street and available to the walking wounded, but, if we found ourselves under sudden siege, we'd be able to retreat and barricade the double doors behind us.

Outside, a grey day. The faithful were garbled together, waiting and restless on the lawn. A fight erupted at the back of the crowd as two burly, bearded guys set about ripping one another new assholes—literally from the sound of it—while everyone else either pretended nothing was happening or egged on the combatants. I watched, Charles watched, we all watched. Drawn by the smell of violence, strangers kept drifting up, alternately bold and fearful, until the audience was about two hundred strong.

I've given some serious thought as to how I should present the speech—or speeches (in the end I spoke three times)—I gave while under Charles' leathery wing. I think the best way will be to include it as a text. Some of it was improvised, much of it came from the introduction to *Nod*, and bits of it—the shrill and polemical bits—came highly recommended by Charles. My words varied slightly with each reiteration, but not that much.

'What has happened is no accident!' Charles was waving my manuscript back and forth. 'It all makes sense and this man,' here he dragged me forward, 'this man wrote it all down before the curse of sleep ended, before we Awoke! It's good news!'

The crowd went completely still, so that the bored screaming of the seagulls was the only sound until I began to speak:

Is this a surprise? If so, ask yourself what you imagined would happen when the old world died— or you did. Did you imagine some lame Heaven where you'd be kissed up to by hosts of angels fascinated by all your wonderful qualities? Would there be better food in the Afterworld? Better sex? Better television? Looking around you today, are you ready to admit that, at the very least, you lacked imagination?

Where did you think you were two weeks ago? In a place called 'Vancouver'? On a planet called 'Earth'? Did you really think those words named something real? Well, they didn't. It was just a story—a story we told one another and agreed to believe in. We looked at the people around us and agreed to call each other 'brother' and 'lover' and 'friend' and 'boss'. And we felt these agreements made us permanent. And we cared about hockey and democracy and phone bills. And we clung to those words like a barnacle clings to a rock.

And so we went from sunrise to sunrise, slipping in and out of sleep [I quickly learned to pause here for a round of teeth gnashing] *but never once thinking that there was anything more to this 'world' of ours than kneeling buses and ghost friends on our computers and fat-free cookies.*

But we were wrong. There was a lot more to the world than that: there were a lot more words out there. There was Nod.

Nod was always out there, always peeking around a corner and watching us. In poverty. In the misfiring DNA of cancer cells. Embedded in the hoodsof drunken SUVs that ploughed down innocent children. But now the pretending is over! Nod is the full meal deal, the director's cut of the world with all the ugly, nasty bits put back in. It's not a world for cowards. It's not a world for the weak. There are demons here in Nod, and monsters, and giant spires that poke through the sky. Eight mile high mushrooms. Flaming swords and Brazen Heads. Anything you can imagine. Angels walking through the alleys, demons beckoning from the shadows.

Nod is what we've been given. It's what we deserve. We'd better get used to it.

When I finished, Charles stepped forward to make his plea for brotherhood and unity among the cracked masses, but for a good five minutes they wouldn't listen, just kept whooping and stomping for me. I'd taken the hard, bitter line, and they'd looked around them and seen a hard, bitter world. The scene playing out in front of us looked like the mosh pit at a punk rock festival in some deeply damaged Eastern European country. As he watched, Charles kept his smile in play, but when he glanced sideways at me, beneath his contorted red face I could glimpse a rawer and even redder one, a flayed face. A flaying face.

Eventually, the mob simmered and Charles spoke some more, growing larger as he began by reciting lines from Nod—or, more properly, a passage from Genesis, as quoted in my manuscript:

'And Cain went out from the face of the Lorde and dwelt in the lande Nod on the east syde of Eden. We are the race of Cain, all of us. But good news! The punishment is now complete! The barren old world of our wanderings is now over. Here in Nod we're called on to establish the new Eden. The old world ended in Fire—did you see the flash? But did you hear what Nodgod said at that moment? I did!'

And so on—the standard evangelical pitch. After Charles finished, most of the crowd stayed for the metaphorical juice and cookies; after all, they had nowhere else to go that didn't involve being alone, hungry, and homi- or suicidal.

It began to rain gently, and nobody except me seemed to notice that the drops that ran down over my upper lip and into my mouth tasted funny. Neither had anyone else seemed to notice the slimy grey film that had begun appearing on white surfaces. Later that afternoon when I crouched in a remote corner of the playground and took my first shit in three days, my stool was crayon yellow.

While Charles' people, Tanya among them, began to shepherd the newcomers toward the school, Charles himself wasted no time dragging me back inside, to a dim corner where no one could see or hear us.

'What was that, Paul?' Something new in his eyes. Fear, I hoped.

'What?'

'The way you spoke.'

'I did what you asked. Charles.'

My little power play was blatant. I knew I'd succeeded beyond his wildest dreams, my secret weapon having been the fact that I didn't give a damn about a world that didn't give a damn about human beings: my contempt had spoken to the crowd. Now Charles would have to deal with the fallout—with the Seattle in my words—if he wanted to keep the spotlight focussed on him.

'You're good with words, Paul. But of course that's not news.' His self-mastery was impressive, despite the wildness of his eyes and the slack condition of his skin. 'I don't mind if you call me by my old Sleeper name when we're alone, Paul, but you need to know that we're renaming everyone out there. New Eden. Take up where Adam left off.'

'Save it for your zombies, Charles.'

He reddened three times. First shade, anger. Second shade, rage. Third shade, the strain of repression of said rage.

'Are we done here?' I asked. 'Or am I still your prisoner?'

My mind flew, on paper wings, to the Book Room and perched there.

'Give me my thousand. Then you can go.'

But go where? Through the hundred kilometre gauntlet of suburbs that sprawled to the east? North toward the mob on the Lion's Gate Bridge? South toward the mushroom cloud? West into haunted, hunted Demon Park? No. Charles' plan would be that I'd go straight to martyrdom, skewered on a kebab stick. There's a natural point in the development of any religion where the prophet becomes first a nuisance and then a positive liability. Just imagine Jesus walking into an evangelical church while the collection plate was being passed around—or into a Catholic priest's chamber while the altar boy's frock is pulled up over his head. At some point it's inevitable that the prophet has to go. When you stop and think about it, that's the take-home message of the entire New Testament: off the prophet.

The rules were set, then. Zoe and I had until Charles got his 'thousand', whatever that was.

'A thousand? Why not? I've always liked round numbers. Charlie.'

And I left him there, swallowing, swallowing.

Pacing the halls that day, I was both famous and feared. The two states are inextricably linked; the famous always have the power to negate the existence of the non-famous in much the same way a light bulb takes out unwary moths—unthinking annihilation in the face of what Rainer Maria Rilke called, referring to angels, 'overwhelming existence'. Charles had lifted me up in the eyes of his followers, and I had to be grateful for that. The haggard Awakened Uriahed and Heeped all over me as I passed by; they Pecked and they Sniffed. When people crawl, they always remind me of Dickensian grotesques. His novels were Nod-like with their small contingents of 'normal' people constantly under siege from the massed hordes of the twisted and absurd. The hard thing when reading a Dickens novel is to keep faith with the normal, not to be seduced and swept away by the freak show.

All in all, being feared suited my mood; I wore my new role gladly, like armour donned against the assaults of my own heart. As I strode through my day, I felt my face adjust to its new role of prophet: my chin rose, my cheeks drew down, and my eyebrows tightened and drew nearer one another. And then, when I turned a corner and found myself alone, I would laugh.

At myself, and a little too intensely for my own liking. Then I'd frown, then laugh again: dizzy circles of me, spinning around.

I made sure that Zoe was fed and watered. She seemed the same as always, content to play with her bear and other toys she'd found in the classroom's cupboards. She was goodness and sweetness, but I could only watch her wordless world from a distance. I was alone and would have to get used to it as best I could.

So long I was able to maintain my status as Rice Jesus, I was confident that I didn't need to fear for Zoe's safety: no one would dare enter our classroom without permission. No one would question why I chose to keep a 'demon' there either. The fermenting imaginations of the Awakened would fill in any gaps left lying around. There were no more gnawing questions in anybody's mind: just a plethora of fantastical answers, gnawing away.

Twelve more days until the Awakened were mostly dead and those who remained would be so incapacitated that they'd be incapable of hunting anything, and Zoe would be safe. We were pretty much half way there, and the odds were that Charles' little kingdom was the safest place to pass at least a few more of those days.

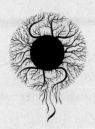

DAY 10
PROCRUSTES' BED

A robber of Attica, who placed all who fell into his hands upon an iron bed. If they were longer than the bed, he cut off the redundant part; if shorter, he stretched them until they fit it.

Planning aside, the next night I pushed my newly-minted luck—rolled that golden coin down those empty hallways toward the screams that echoed out from Captain America's cell. His anguish had become more than I could ignore, and my thoughts first built a nest then roosted outside the closet at the back of the bookroom.

For the last couple of nights I'd noticed that my thoughts were turning more and more toward the Dream. It was like a physical craving. The Dream was gravity, bending my thoughts in its direction so that every one of the dozens of problems I faced seemed as though they would be most easily solved through the closing of my eyes. Each time I slept the pull was greater, the return to Nod more difficult. In fact, I was beginning to worry that each night's sleep might be the one that never ended, the one that left Zoe alone in Charles' dark world.

And yet, the more the Dream drew me toward it, the more I also became aware of what my fellow Sleeper was going through, awake for days on end. By comparison, the stabbing of skewers seemed a trivial thing.

Captain America's pitiable cries were even affecting the otherwise unflappable Zoe. Indeed, this was the first thing I'd seen affect her in any way, despite the fact that she'd already seen the full menu of 'things no child should ever see'—but which, we adults conveniently forget, they actually see all the time. Children are the eternal, silent witnesses to every human sin, and the more we tatter their purity, the more we extol the clean white blouses of 'innocence'. Already during her short spell inside our fractured narratives, Zoe had seen both Tanya's terrible descent and my wallowing in the muddy bottom of that fall; she'd seen spooky, twisted shapes at every corner.

When Captain America cried out, Zoe didn't start or cry, but she stopped in her solitary play and looked down into her lap for a moment or two, the lack of expression on her soft, still-babyish face itself a kind of expression.

The rescue mission I now found myself contemplating was tricky. There was no predictable ebb or flow to life among the Awakened, no supper or bedtimes. The structure, such as it was, was all based around intense focus on individual tasks, both mundane and esoteric. Charles' Awakened worked furiously and continually, mostly scrubbing and wiping, conjuring and praying. That afternoon I'd passed three of them gathered around an old yellow typewriter someone had dragged up from the basement. They took turns hitting random keys, eyes shut tight. After a few minutes of this, they pulled out their sheet of paper and crowded together by a broken window, anxious to see what wisdom they'd transcribed, presumably from the mouth of Nodgod. As they scanned the page, their faces twisted and fell.

To my mind, it seemed likely that the Awakened were speeding up the rate of their own decay and death through their efforts. But what did I care about that? It was the same before, when people would warn about the inevitability of environmental destruction (now looking to be reversed, assuming too many more nukes don't go off before they rust away). *Conserve, conserve*, they'd whinny, knowing full well that their anaemic efforts would never make an ounce of difference. For myself, I'd always muttered, *consume, consume,* reasoning that the sooner we hit the crisis point, the sooner we'd be forced to stop shitting where we ate.

The practical point here is that there was no natural time at which to stage a daring rescue of the good Captain. There would be no sleepy-headed guards at midnight, no lunch-bloated siestas in the afternoon. One time was as good as another, and so I decided to make my attempt when Zoe fell asleep.

I tucked her in, grizzly on guard, then wrote and pinned a large note to the classroom door, threatening every sort of revenge I could imagine (An Iron Maiden! Procrustes' Bed! The Dread Horrors of the Oubliette! All that good dungeon stuff) on anyone who might dare disturb her slumber.

Back in the book room, I stopped and listened at the door. Hearing nothing but that head-roar we optimistically call silence, I gingerly turned the knob and went inside.

A single candle flickered. Both prisoner and guard looked eagerly up, each hungry for a break in their common drudgery of stimulus/response. How many days had they been trapped in here together? Captain America seemed to be melting into the floor, and I wondered if he'd begun to welcome the periodic stab of that skewer as a blessed release from the monotony.

Three buckets brim-full of shit and piss stood in one corner; a couple of empty cans and a milk jug filled with murky water stood in another. I gagged and looked up. The ceiling was high enough to be invisible in the faint light. I looked back down and found Captain America's eyes locked on mine.

'I'm Paul.'

'My name's—'

Skewer Lady screeched, obscuring whatever he said next.

'No! He's a liar! His name is *Rag*!'

The three syllable version of 'rag', I should note. I turned on her.

'No. He still has his old name, just like I do and just like you do, *Judy*.'

She mumbled words that never made it out of her closed mouth.

'What did you say?'

She spoke to the floor. 'My name is Gytrash.'

I tried not to laugh but let out a smirk. Gytrash, a northern

English spirit that waylaid travellers caught on the road too late at night.

'Gytrash. Okay. Gytrash, I've come for 'Rag'. The Admiral wants him downstairs.'

'No!'

'The Admiral wants you to stay here and be ready when he comes back.'

She scowled and shook her head.

This was going nowhere. I grabbed her and pushed her against the wall. She began to laugh.

'You can stop me, but you can't stop the Rabbit Hunt. Can't save the demon children...'

'What do you mean?'

Skewer Lady just giggled to herself. 'Can't save the demons! Can't save their souls!'

'What is a Rabbit Hunt?' It wasn't a phrase from *Nod*.

Her voice took on a sing-songy tone. 'The Admiral will take a Thousand...drive the demons into the sea. Admiral hates dreamy little heads going to pull their bodies from the water and let us drink their blood...'

Spying a roll of duct tape hanging from a nail, I grabbed it, ripped off a piece and plastered it haphazardly across her mouth. She tried to stab at me with her skewer, but I pulled it from her hand and threw it away. I hadn't given any thought to what to do about her when I stole her prisoner.

She kept babbling through the tape, which didn't completely cover her mouth. I could only pick out and guess at random words as I tore off another piece and applied it.

'Juggle…leaves…stop…shining…wave…stop…' It was like an emergency broadcast from a group of hysterical Fridge Magnet poets.

Finally, I simply took the whole roll and wound it around her head three or four times. That silenced her. She just sat there on the floor looking ridiculous. I turned my attention toward Captain America.

'Let's get you out of here.' I was in full comic book action mode now.

'Out of where?' he asked, tears blackening the grey fabric of his filthy T-shirt. 'There's nowhere to go. I just want to sleep…'

A set of keys hung beside the door, just beyond his reach. I tried one after another on the U-shaped bike lock that chained his neck to the pipe until it clicked and opened.

'Get up.'

He shook his head. I went over to Gytrash, pulled her over to the pipe as gently as I could, and locked her duct-taped head to the pipe while she struggled feebly, animal growls emerging from beneath the tape.

Captain America still wasn't moving, so I slapped him. 'Get *up*!'

He staggered upright.

'Now listen. When we leave the book room, there's a stairwell directly across the hall. Two flights down and we'll reach an exit into an alley. You understand?'

He nodded.

'Let's go.'

I needn't have bothered with the rescue drama. When we went out into the hall there were a only few of the Awakened scattered up and down its length, illuminated by dim candlelight. A couple of them glanced up as we passed, but none showed any interest.

We made it to the alley without encountering anyone else.

'Where are we going?' Captain America moaned. 'There's nowhere to go!'

A good point. I had no idea where we were going. My goal had been a simple one: to get him out of the school. Now that I'd accomplished it, I might as well have turned around and gone back inside for all the ideas I had left.

'Is there anywhere you want to go?'

He began to cry again.

'Tell me your name again, man.' I always appreciate the efficacy of a quick 'man' when it comes to creating instant intimacy. I could pull off a 'man', but never, quite, a 'dude'.

'Brandon. But there's nowhere to go.'

'Don't be stupid, Brandon. Anywhere is better than where you were. Listen, here's the deal. I can get you away from here to somewhere where you can sleep for a few hours. Are you listening? Then when you wake up, you'll be able to think more clearly and consider your options. Okay?'

He nodded slightly.

'Now pay attention and make sure you process this. You only have to survive for another two weeks, tops, until these maniacs are all dead. Do you remember hearing that on the news before the power went out? Do you understand?' I shook him by the shoulders for emphasis. 'Two weeks or less.'

Still nothing but silence from Captain Brandon, so I played my last and best card. 'When we find you a safe place, you can sleep. And have the dream.'

His head shot up and his eyes locked on mine. They were blazing.

We padded down the alley until we reached a street that ran south, straight toward the beach. Above English Bay, the moon was obscured by a stray cloud. In the distance, a glimmer of liquorice ocean, framed by the mould-black outlines of arbutus trees. Stray dogs, usually so deferential during the day, came closer, cowered less. Ahead of us squatted a string of three and four storey apartment buildings, mute toad sentries. Trees arched over our heads, entwining their branches to obscure the stars. And quiet—a keening quiet made of listening ears—all around us.

'What was that?'

Beside me, Brandon's eyes were large and liquid as they stared. I heard it too: a low thrumming.

'Watch out! Watch out!'

A shape scurried between us, so stooped as to appear to be running on all fours. Then, as quickly as it had appeared, the figure burrowed back into the blackness.

'What the fuck was that?' Brandon demanded, his voice shaking.

'Just one of them.'

'No. It wasn't human. It was a rat. A giant rat,' he said, as though trying to stuff his foot into a much-too-small shoe. His hands were quarrelling.

'It wasn't a rat.' I affected scorn, but didn't feel it. In the shadows of my memory a giant rodent appeared as I rewound and replayed the last ten seconds. It was the Blemmye incident all over again. In Nod, words were highly infectious. Nod itself was literally a plague of words. I was going to have to be careful about what I thought, what I said.

We sleepwalked toward the beach. The thrumming grew and as it did, other sounds were slowly becoming discernible in the mix. Sounds that suggested images. I began to see shapes in the distance.

'I need to sleep,' Brandon moaned, but he meant dream. Then somehow he was flat on his back in the middle of the street, staring up at the trees and I was standing over him. 'Tell me who to pray to.'

'I don't know.'

'Is it death?' he asked.

'What?'

'The dream. Do you think the dream is death?'

'I don't know.'

Brandon looked up at me and smiled. 'You've got to laugh. If it's death, then it's okay. If the dream is death, then we're safe. I hope it's death. I hope I die. I'm ready to die."

'Who were you, Brandon? Before?'

He raised himself up on one elbow. 'Who was I?'

'Before.'

'I don't know. I was...I was a bus driver. Was that what you wanted to know? Then for a while I was a fucking dart board for some crazy old bitch.' He laughed and shook his head. 'And now I'm lying on the road. Oh, man, I just need to close my eyes for five minutes...'

The sounds from up ahead were pulling apart from one another, taking on individual identities. Squawks and squeals. Roaring and chattering. Some sort of mob scene.

I grabbed Brandon and dragged him to his feet. Odd shadows were feeding in from the alleys and buildings around us, all heading in the same direction.

And suddenly, there we were. The beach. A mass of black shapes; a black mass of shapes.

My head spun. I had to wonder if, after three days with virtually no sleep, I was beginning to see some of the same things Tanya and Charles saw. If so, then Nod was a far more terrible place than I'd imagined. Before us was a fantastic monochromatic scene, populated by creatures both real and mythical. Writhing pythons, massive, knot-shouldered apes. I recognized a Gandaberunda, the double-headed bird from Hindu mythology; a Cretan Bull or Gyuki with enormous, hollow eyes that glowed like moons. Massive crabs, pincers clicking, and enormous spiders, spike-stepping on the sand.

Ever kick at a mound of dirt and expose an ant's nest? That was the nature of the motion on the beach that night. Part sock hop, part orgy, part pitched battle—the beach was swarming with impossibilities. Ever close your eyes and pay close attention to the shapes that squirm behind your lids? That was what I saw. What I thought I saw. What I saw. So little light, so much black canvas for my mind to splatter. A contact high, perhaps, with the minds of a thousand maniacs.

Then a gibbous moon emerged from behind its cloud and revealed even more. A brutal democracy of size: giant, sharp-beaked robins and dwarf elephants; miniature dinosaurs and massive cockroaches and slugs. And they were busy. Fucking and fighting, cawing and screeching. Like what amphetamine-fuelled punk rockers and orgiastic Romans had *thought* they were doing, but now for real. That was the moment when Hieronymus Bosch came into sharp focus for me as a steely-eyed realist. A gorilla was riding a hysterical, bleating fawn while a pair of giant, grinning frogs panted approval and a six-foot tall raccoon stood on its hind legs, watching as it licked its slick and dripping paws, a huge erection clearly visible between its legs. Three giant house cats lapped at the goopy innards of a torn-open scorpion, its stinger still twitching above their heads.

But surely these weren't really animals, but people? I turned to look at Brandon and saw, looking back at me, a massive blinking squirrel in a filthy Captain America T-shirt, its head flitting back and forth, its muzzle twitching in terror. And then I looked slowly down.

I saw my body covered in shaggy fur; I held up my arms and saw the stubby paws and long, straight claws of what could only be a grizzly bear.

Then a shape appeared on the sidewalk beside me. Another bear—a black one—its muzzle inches from my own face.

'What do you want?' I asked.

'What do you want?' the creature mimicked me, its voice a stoned drone.

I tried to step around it. 'Get out of my way.'

'Get out of my way.' The creature blocked my path. Its gums were black in the moonlight, its sharp teeth burning white. Every move I made, the bear mimicked until I began to think it must be my mirror image. Then I reached my paw out and felt fur. At that same moment, the other creature's claws raked my chest, and I felt blood trickling down like sweat.

'Say, 'I'm walking away now'', squirrel-Brandon chattered into my ear.

'I'm walking away now.'

'I'm walking away now,' my mirror repeated.

As I backed up, followed closely by squirrel-Brandon, so did my doppelganger. Eventually, it lost interest in us, dropped down onto all fours, and loped back into the melee.

We crossed Beach Avenue and stepped onto the sand. Directly ahead of us, a pack of howling chimpanzees held down a squirming, bloodied kitten, its four broken limbs painfully splayed outwards. When it struggled, loud grinding sounds emanated from the broken bones beneath its skin. All around, other creatures were throwing rocks at the poor creature, or slashing at it with their claws. Helplessly, we moved toward the scene.

An albino crow was hopping back and forth in front of the writhing kitten, its beak opening and shutting, its eyes milky and pupil-less. As we approached, the creature was bobbing its head and speaking into the kitten's ear.

'There, there, there. It won't hurt much longer. Soon you'll be asleep.'

Behind me, Brandon whimpered.

'The bag!'

In response to the crow's words, a grinning chimpanzee threw a black plastic garbage bag over the kitten's head and held it tight around the poor creature's neck. The bag huffed and puffed as the kitten struggled. Then it went limp.

The crow ordered the bag removed. Exposed, the fur on the kitten's head was matted and damp.

'Are you sleeping?' the crow whispered into its ear.

The kitten's head moved a little. This upset the crow, which began to hop back and forth in fury.

'Get the dream stick!' it screamed. The nearest chimp picked up a hefty piece of driftwood with a large knot like an eye on one end. 'I try to help you! I try and try and try to help you sleep! And you won't do it!'

The chimp smashed the kitten on the crown of its head, then paused, panting, to consider the effects of its actions.

'Are you sleeping?' the crow moved in, gentle and solicitous once again.

No response.

'Is it still breathing?'

The chimpanzee loped over and put its ear to the kitten's mouth.

'Fuck, no,' it replied with some satisfaction. 'It's dead.'

As the animals that had been holding the kitten down faded away into the background, the crow flew into a rage and began pecking viciously at the corpse. It was more than I could handle.

'Leave it alone!'

The crow turned and aimed its bloody beak at me. 'Stay out of the Lord's work!'

The giant crow hopped toward me, stopping only when we were eye to eye. Twinned eyes, something all creatures share.

'I helped it repent. So it should have been able to sleep! I do what I can to help, but nothing is ever good enough!' Then the crow's voice took on a resigned tone. 'But it's out of my hands now.'

'What hands?' I asked, but the crow ignored me.

Though its face was incapable of showing human emotion, the crow sounded mournful when it spoke again. 'Everything's gone. At night, we're not even human in the eyes of the Lord any more. We're nothing but shadows. There's a lesson we're failing to learn. But what? It's a school and we're failing.'

'But what if you're wrong? What if there's no reason for any of this? What if it's just happening?'

The crow's eyes glinted. 'You're crazy. Crazy. We're in a maze of paying, and the only way out is to figure out what for and how much. We can't be forgiven if we don't know what we've done. What have we done? What have we done? What...?'

A commotion up by the water stopped the crow's reverie, and the crowd began to surge forward. We were pulled along with everyone else until we were reached the shore. Then I saw something I never thought I'd see again: the steady glow of electric lights far out in English Bay. A grid of unblinking white. It could only have been one thing: a ship. A big one.

As we stared at those piercing points of light, our animal shapes fell away from us and we reverted to our tattered human forms.

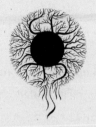

DAY 11
CAT'S SLEEP

A sham sleep, like that of a cat watching a mouse.

'Rise and shine, pal. Rise and shine.'

And I did rise, ever so slowly. Ever so reluctantly. I opened my eyes into blazing morning sunlight so bright as to almost be a sound. My first feeling was shock at realizing I'd slept. Then I went straight into Zoe-directed heart palpitations. Where was I? I wasn't at the school, which meant that Zoe was alone and had been all night. Or longer.

'You too.'

I turned over and saw a boot-shod foot prodding Brandon's shoulder. A shiny, well-polished boot—something whole in a shattered world. But Brandon didn't wake up; he just turned onto his other side and pressed his face up against a sheet of cardboard, one, I now remembered, that we'd threaded through the railings last night to conceal our hiding place.

Then it all came back to me. After leaving the beach, we'd climbed onto the first floor balcony of this empty apartment and broken its French doors open. We'd hoped to pass the night in there, but the swaths of dried blood we'd found on the walls and floors forced us back outside.

Below us, the Awakened were muttering and wandering. The arrival of the mystery ship had shaken them up. I could almost feel the effort that was going into assimilation—in trying to gag down the fact of electric lights out there in English Bay along with all the slippery new mythologies they were all still choking on. What, I couldn't help but wonder, would Charles make of this latest jigsaw piece? And more importantly, what did I make of it? Was the ship crewed by people who'd figured out a cure for the insomnia epidemic? Had the cavalry arrived?

As soon as we'd put up our cardboard barrier, Brandon flopped down to the floor. He fell asleep almost instantly, but not before saying one final word to me in a gentle, relieved voice: 'Goodbye.'

'You. Do something with him. Wake him up.'

Back in the present, a strong hand grabbed the back of my T-shirt and hoisted me into a sitting position.

My captor—what else could he have been?—was a short, muscular man with a neatly trimmed black beard. But it was his clothes I was looking at. They were shockingly clean, just like his boots. In fact, his khaki pants and white T-shirt looked brand new, as did the gleaming rifle slung over his shoulder. This was the first person I'd seen in eleven days who looked like what normal had once been, if that's not too tortuous a way to put it.

'Are you from the ship?' I asked.

He ignored me and pointed at Brandon.

'Wake him up now. Don't make me ask again.'

I pushed Brandon's shoulder with the palm of my hand, but to no avail.

'I don't know why he's not waking up. He hadn't slept for days, I know that. He was tortured.'

Strange to be speaking openly of sleep again.

'Roll him onto his back.'

'Are you from that ship in English Bay?'

He spat and shook his head.

'Nah, I'm from over by Main and Quebec. Just flip him over.'

I did, but just like the Cowardly Lion in the poppy fields of Oz, there was no rousing poor Captain America. Our new friend ground his teeth as he looked up and down the street.

'God damn it. We can't carry him all the way across town. God damn it.'

I fell easily into the rhythm of my captor's baffled logic. 'Well, if we can't move him, we'd better hide him.'

He nodded, and so we dragged Brandon's limp body inside the apartment, reasoning to one another as we did so that A) the place had already been looted and was unlikely to be a target for scavengers and B) the quantity of dried blood on display would be a turnoff for all but the most deranged of the Awakened.

We managed to stash Brandon behind a futon that, seen from the apartment door, concealed him fairly well. If anyone entered from the balcony, though, it would be game over. With this in mind, Dave—during our exertions we'd exchanged names—suggested we leave the interior door open.

'What now?' I asked.

He made the frowny face some people use to indicate serious thought: chin up, jowls down. And while he thought-grimaced, I studied him. Despite his admirable grooming, Dave was one of the Awakened—there was no doubt of that now that I'd had a good look at him. No matter how clean he kept himself, there was no disguising the black rings beneath his eyes and the cadaverous expression he wore. Although he'd tried.

The strangest thing about Dave was this: despite being a poster child for macho guerrilla chic, he was wearing makeup. Lots of makeup. Foundation and cover up, if my memory of female grooming habits serves me well. The effect was the exact opposite of what Tanya had tried to do with me before we went into the park: plausibly pre-Nod at twenty feet or more. Up close, however, Dave looked like an ageing soap opera Lothario. A perfect phrase popped into my mind: Cat's sleep. Cat's sleep is sham sleep: the sort that your household tabby will feign while surveilling a mouse. Dave was a Cat Sleeper.

Having finished thinking he relaxed his face. 'I'm taking you back to the base. We'll come back for your friend tonight if Dr London decides that's the plan.'

'But what if I've got somewhere else I need to be?'

To his credit, Dave had the good manners not to stare significantly at his rifle. Instead he rubbed his temples with his thumbs as he spoke.

'We Sleepers have got to stick together. It's a fucking nightmare out there, man. As I'm sure you well know.'

To his credit, Dave had walking through Nod down to a science. For the most part we stayed, abandoned cars permitting, in the exact centre of the street. He cradled his rifle, its barrel pointing the way forward—a clear statement of intent that no one we encountered was eager to dispute. He moved quickly but not so quickly as to create an impression of haste. Purposefulness was the name of his game.

I followed close behind.

We cut straight through the heart of the West End, passing within a block of Charles' School, then turned up Robson and entered the urban canyon that led toward Granville Street and the heart of downtown. Until then, the streets had been quiet; all we'd seen were flitting shadows and the occasional blood-muzzled dog. It was a comfortable, familiar apocalypse, something I'd seen rehearsed in a hundred or more big budget movies: burned cars, ragged curtains fluttering through broken windows.

Soon enough, though, we came across a bizarre sight, even by Noddish standards. Directly ahead of us people were emerging from their hidey holes and gathering in the middle of the street. We stopped to watch as they gathered together, all of them staring straight up into the sky, faces open as sunflowers. Some grinned and laughed at whatever it was they thought they were seeing, while others held their hands over their mouths in amazement, joyous tears trickling down their cheeks. I looked up and saw nothing but blue sky and a few wispy clouds.

In a minute there were fifty people. In another minute there'd be a hundred.

'What the hell is going on?' Dave asked. He'd looked up for a second but was now keeping his red-rimmed eyes fixed on the pavement. He looked terrified.

Emboldened by my companion's big brother of a gun, I went up to a particularly ecstatic young woman who had deep, infected scratches running up and down her arms. Two weeks ago, she would have been gorgeous: model-thin and fine-boned. Now she was a tottering skeleton, walking on tiptoes, as though in high heels, even though her feet were bare and bloodied.

'What is it?' I asked.

'Can't you see?' she said rapturously. 'It's the angels! There are thousands of angels flying across the sky! It's going to be okay! They're here to save us!'

I went and reported back to Dave.

He kept his head down and spat again. 'It's just more of their crazy ass bullshit. This sort of thing was happening all the time yesterday. I heard people talking about a fountain of silver water that was supposed to have appeared out front of the museum. They said if you drank it you'd be able to read minds. Don't listen to the poor bastards—it'll just fuck with your head.'

The woman I'd spoken to followed us as we began to move slowly through the crowd.

'Don't you see them?' she cried, sincerely sorry for us. 'The angels are coming! Oh, thank God…thank God!'

What were they seeing? I suspected the little sperm-like squiggles we all see when we stare up into a bright blue sky: amoeba angels swimming across the surface of our eyeballs.

Meanwhile, Dave kept glowering at the asphalt, his face growing more and more furious. He was the engineer on some runaway train of thought, barrelling toward a destination I wasn't particularly interested in visiting.

'Watch this.' He turned and faced the angel-watchers, smiling grimly. Cupping his hands around his mouth, and without even bothering to try to sound like he meant it, he yelled, 'Holy shit! Those aren't angels. They're devils!'

The effect was instantaneous. There isn't much distance, once you're forced to think about it, between a smile and a grimace of terror. Just two slightly different sets of facial contortions. On the street behind us, a hundred expressions shifted, and we all entered yet another hell. A man began to scream in a little girl voice while the skeleton woman dropped to her knees, still gazing upward, and began to deepen the wounds on her forearms with ragged fingernails. Within seconds, the rest had followed suit, falling to the ground and grovelling among the glass. I began to turn away in horror, but one screamed word stopped me even as it froze everyone else within range.

'Satan!'

The hundred or so haggard figures seemed made of grey stone, all of them fixed by four limbs to the ground. Two hundred eyes swivelled, locking on the solitary figure of a muscular young man with a shaved head and a ring of black tattoos around his neck. He had just emerged, shirtless, from the shattered front window of a boutique, stepping through a thicket of toppled and denuded mannequins, a two litre bottle of Diet Coke clutched in his right hand. He stopped and surveyed the scene.

A hundred shaking arms lifted and pointed at him.

My first impression was that he was someone who had been an arrogant prick. His tattoos and his gym-moulded body spoke of someone devoted to the dark arts of public presentation. Or maybe those were just my flabby prejudices showing through.

'Satan…' A hundred whispers wavered, finding an odd sort of harmony in a drawn-out recitation of that name.

The tattooed man stood there surrounded by a briar patch of empty gestures formed by the mannequins' hands and elbows, grinning and listening as the crowd murmured. His head jerked slightly up and down as he appeared to give his attention to an entire parliament of disembodied advisors. Then a decision was made.

Dropping the bottle and splaying his hands far apart, he showed the crowd his palms.

'I…'

'Let's get out of here,' I whispered.

Dave shook his head. All the tension had fled from his face; his storm had passed, and he stood beside me, muscular arms crossed across his chest, an oasis of calm.

'Nah. This should be fun.'

'Satan…' the crowd hissed.

'…am…'

'Satan…' They willed him forward.

'...Lucifer!' he cried, then laughed hysterically. He leaned forward, hands on his knees, and shook his head. 'Fucking A! Oh, why didn't I see it sooner?! Kiss the dirt, you motherfucking pieces of...'

A cracking sound almost deafened me as Dave raised his rifle and shot. The newly-minted Lucifer fell amid the naked mannequins, and the mob recommenced its worm-frenzy.

'Why did you—?'

'Ah, fuck him. Let's go. We've got miles to go before we sleep, my friend.'

To my—literally—shell-shocked ears, his voice sounded like it came from a long, long way away.

Eventually we came to the very familiar SkyTrain station on Granville Street. Its wide, shady entrance had, until recently, been favoured by beggars and buskers. Now a pile of dead bodies lay in the entrance, flies buzzing around them in the dimness like a thousand invisible electric shavers. All the dead appeared to have been killed by a single bullet to the forehead. The message wasn't hard to read: attempt entry and die.

Dave whistled loudly three times. Someone inside whistled back, and we went in.

Seen from the street, the entrance was a black hole, but once we were inside the foyer, I could make out a string of flickering candles marking the way further in toward the escalators that led down to the station platforms below. Ahead of us, four men and a woman, each as impeccably dressed as Dave, crouched behind sand bag piles, rifles at the ready.

One man with a gaunt, severe face, came out from behind the barricade and spoke to Dave, ignoring me.

'Who's he?'

'One of us. I found him over on Beach Avenue.'

'Let's see him.'

He came close, took out a flashlight, and shined it into my eyes for a long time. He was wearing the same makeup as Dave, and he had the same careful watchfulness about him.

Satisfied, he stepped back, jerking his head toward the dead escalators that led a couple of hundred feet further underground. A chill, blindfolded wind was feeling its way up from the tracks beneath, seeking warmth.

'Okay. Go on.'

More candles lit the way as we stumbled down the escalator.

The platform, when we reached it, was completely dark, but Dave pulled out a flashlight then hopped onto the tracks and shone his beam down the eastbound tunnel. He gestured for me to follow, but I flinched, thinking of the third rail, that bright yellow bar of electricity that we'd all feared as we'd waited for our inventions to pick us up and whisk us away.

Our inventions had sometimes demanded sacrifices. Trains, for example, would occasionally take their tribute in the form of certain unlucky individuals—depressed moms and stoned teenagers, mostly. Such sacrifices were built in. I mean, think about it. How hard would it have been to design barriers that would have made it impossible for people to jump or fall onto the tracks? But we hadn't bothered; we'd been willing to accept a little blood for the sake of our economical and efficient train gods.

Dave was growing more and more impatient. 'Stop daydreaming and get your ass down here.'

I sat down on the edge of the platform and hopped onto the track, avoiding the yellow rail. Dave snorted and, directing his beam downward, stamped on it with his boot-shod foot.

'It's dead. There's nothing to be frightened of. Man up, buddy.'

I nodded at the beam, which had now swung up to probe my face.

'You don't believe me? Just touch it.'

'That's okay.'

'Touch it.'

Taking a deep breath, I reached down and did as he ordered, holding my breath. Somewhere above me, Dave laughed.

And so we marched into the eastbound tunnel, the sea breeze at our backs.

'Next station…Science World,' Dave said, mimicking the voice and cadence of the SkyTrain system's now-defunct automated announcement system. 'No monsters down here, pal. They're all up there in the daylight. This tunnel is secure. Just walk with one foot dragging along the right rail. That'll keep you oriented. Stadium Station is just a half a click ahead. Then we'll be back in the daylight. What a day. Man, I'm ready for some shut eye.'

It took us about a half an hour to cover the distance. Stadium is the point on the downtown line where the tracks emerge from underground just outside BC Place and begin their elevated course across town, bathed in a tsunami of light I couldn't even begin to imagine from down there.

Daylight first appeared in the distance as a tiny, bobbing cousin to Dave's flashlight beam, but it quickly grew and stabilized. When we emerged from the tunnel, we found Stadium Station fortified and manned by a dozen or so more Daves, both male and female. Their makeup genericized them, almost comically, as with some dance troupe or rock video where uniformity in appearance and motion is considered the hallmark of something avant garde. When they saw us, Dave's compatriots nodded but didn't speak. Instead, their attention was turned to the perimeter.

Chain link fencing surrounded the station itself. The barbed wire-topped security perimeter predated our little apocalypse, having been put into place when the line was built in order to keep panhandlers and the suicidal homeless away from the tracks. Outside, a few dozen of the Awakened milled about, weaving in between the bodies of others who'd fallen to the guards' rifles. One man approached the fence with a pleading look and pressed his face against the wire, only to have a woman with a long pony tail and heavy eyebrows smash the butt of her rifle into his nose. He recoiled, howling and bleeding, then fell to the ground.

We passed through the station and began to march along the now-elevated rail, past BC Place and GM Place, the city's two largest arenas. Almost immediately, the streets were fifty feet of falling, flailing dread beneath us. As the Awakened watched us pass over their heads, some screamed obscenities, others prayers. The abuse was clearly audible, but I couldn't make out the words from so high up. I wondered if God experienced similar reception problems up in heaven.

Soon the next station, Science World, appeared ahead of us—a giant geodesic dome that housed an interpretation centre where, until recently, celebrity Tyrannosaurus skeletons had come and gone while kid-friendly magicians taught surreptitious lessons about gravity and math. The dome's glass triangles, winking in the sun, reminded me of the shattered UBC mirrors that had heralded my first foray into the Golden Light.

I spoke to Dave's back.

'Who are you guys?'

Nothing. Apparently it was flatter-the-mad time again.

'You're really organized.'

Nothing. I couldn't have pinned the feeling down just then, but as Dave and I were drawing nearer and nearer to Science World, he was changing. Maybe his back had stiffened when I started asking questions, perhaps his parched brain was emitting some sort of adrenaline frizzle or maybe it was something else entirely. Human beings can snatch fragments of emotion from the air with the same acuity with which a cougar picks up a whiff of deer blood from miles away. However it happened, though, I suddenly realized that if I was smart, I'd stop talking and just follow along.

* * *

Science World, tone-rich in the orange-ing evening sun, turned out to be the last fortified station. Beyond, the rails were populated by the Awakened. Some were dressed in filthy thrift store mimicry of Dave's people—crazy commandos holding plastic dollar store Uzis. Maybe they were mocking the Cat Sleepers, poor mice, or maybe they were auditioning in hopes of joining the cast. Once in a while, one would get too close to the fence. Then, like before, a rifle's patience would snap in two and a rumpled body would tumble in slow motion toward an unheard thud.

Within the compound that had been erected around the dome, however, there was order. Dozens of people, all dressed in that same uniform of khaki pants and T-shirt, strode purposefully about. A fleet of twelve SUVs was parked neatly in one corner. Six trailer trucks, their back doors open, looked to be filled with cases of food. A helicopter stood at the centre of a freshly-painted bull's-eye, ready to take off and be mistaken for an angel or demon by the denizens of Nod.

'What do you call this place?' I asked, sincerely impressed.

He looked disgusted. 'Science World, Paul. What are you on, man? It's called Science World. Quebec Street. Vancouver, British Columbia. Holy fuck, has everyone in the world gone crazy?'

Dr London, when I met him, was a surprise: a fat cat in a world growing leaner by the second. Even before Nod the sight of a stout doctor would have raised at least one if not both of my eyebrows—and London must have tipped the scales at 300 pounds or more. The West Coast doctors I'd known had always been fastidious exercise addicts. It was as though all the dark and terrible secrets of the human body they'd learned in medical school had electro-shocked them into frenetic self-improvement regimes. But not Dr Wallace London.

He was in his early thirties. Thinning blonde hair. Red-cheeks and a double-chin surrounding an embarrassed, teen-aged grin—but a grin I immediately sensed could be vicious, like the fat kid in high school who gets teased and teased and then turns mean.

And so, when Dave presented me to London in the cafeteria, I trod gingerly.

'Good to meet you!' The doctor reached forward and held my left hand between his two damp paws.

'Same here.'

He had a British accent that I was sure was fake before he'd spoken three full sentences. His overall demeanour strove for 'gracious host' but he came across as more charmed than charming. A speckless white lab coat was wrapped around his girth and held in place by a wide white belt. He was a Cat Sleeper, too. They all were.

As he studied my face, Dr London was slowly licking his chops. Round and round, doing the full circle every three or four seconds: his fleshy lips were raw with it. Was he even a doctor? Almost certainly not. It was far more likely that, a couple of weeks ago, 'Dr London' had been living in his parents' basement, strung out on video games and Internet porn. In other words, a kissing cousin to Charles.

'You've got quite the set-up happening here.'

'Thank you. Yes, I'd say we do. Some of us thought we should have made a convoy and headed east into the mountains to wait out the plague. But I disagreed. I felt that we'd want to be here when the madness ended in order to begin to put things back together. In the meantime, we do what we can to make sure those poor, demented bastards out there don't destroy too much. We're a government-in-waiting, if you like. We'll have a jolly difficult time putting things back together as it is, without letting those poor bastards burn the place to the ground first. But they'll be gone soon enough. Right now we kill the ones we can, but our ammunition is limited, so mostly we confine our activities to securing resources and rescuing people like yourself. Our fellow Sleepers.'

As he checked out my reaction I strove not to have one.

The cafeteria was open for business, with food being prepared on propane stoves. Seeing this, I realized how hungry I was and said as much to London. He gestured to one of his troops who went and got me a large bowl of stew and some freshly-baked flat bread.

While I ate, my stomach groaning with relief, London enthused about his plans.

'I assume you've heard of the Four Weeks timetable? Of course you have. One more week and we can begin to take back the city, I think. We'll begin in Chinatown—low density compared to downtown proper—and move west, building by building. Then over the Lion's Gate to the hydro dams on the North Shore. We've got a couple of engineers on the team who'll be able to get the power turned back on. We'll take it all back. A terrible tragedy, by Jove, but we can only hope something stronger will emerge after all these trials.'

He paused and licked his lips some more.

I focussed on my stew and thought fast. London talked about rescuing Sleepers, but I had yet to see a real one here. What did that mean? Looking up, I saw he was giving me a dead-eye stare.

'What's up?' London scowled, his accent slipping. Then he paused, twitched, and reverted to bad-Gatsby mode. 'What do you think about it all, old chap?'

Two men at the next table, rifles slung across their backs, stared at me hard. Think? About what? I hadn't been paying attention. A woman came up and set down two cups of coffee and a small pitcher of cream. As I tried to find the dropped thread of the conversation an odd expression drifted into view on London's face.

'Have you visited Stanley Park recently?' he asked. The question popped out a little too eagerly for my liking. Behind his face, something rattled at a door. I sensed that the correct answer was 'no' and replied accordingly.

London rubbed his neck like a poor orphan boy rubbing a magic lamp. He reddened, and the effect was to cause the makeup around his eyes to look like two poached eggs about to slide down his cheeks.

'Only we hear such strange stories about the park. Have you heard any rumours?'

'Just the usual ones, I guess.'

'Such as…'

'Like about the kids.'

London stopped breathing, as did the rest of the room.

'Yes,' he began again after a moment. 'We've heard similar things. What do you know?'

'The usual stuff. That they sleep but don't talk. That they live in the park. That the Awakened hate them and are hunting them down and killing them.'

Whispers everywhere, spreading like spider webs.

'The Awakened? Is that what you call them?'

'Yes.'

'And that's all you've heard?'

'Yes, I think so.'

My heart was racing and racing but unable to escape the confines of my chest: it understood the danger I had stumbled into better than my poor brain.

London nodded and nodded, all the while stirring his coffee. Up and down. Around and around.

'Would you like to hear what we've heard?'

'Sure.'

He snorted. 'Of course you'd like to hear, old chap. But can we trust you? Can you give me a reason? You are on our side, aren't you? Or maybe you're a spy...'

His accent was almost gone now, and his face was darkening. All around me rifles shifted in sweaty palms. Suddenly I knew why there were no other true Sleepers here: London wanted reasons from the mice he brought home, but all our pockets were full of holes. Still, I had to give him whatever pieces of lint I was able to pinch between my fingers.

'There's one more thing. A group of the Awakened. They've got a plan.'

'A group? What group?' He was getting angry. 'And what plan? Why are you hiding things from us after we've taken you in and fed you? Wh-what are you up to?'

'They're planning to go into the park soon and exterminate the children. They say the kids are demons.'

Uproar all around us. London gasped, but then pulled himself together and raised a hand. Silence fell like a dropped hammer.

'What do you mean, 'exterminate' them?'

'They plan to march through the park and drive the children into the ocean and drown them.'

'Where are these people?!' London was keeping his fury on a choke chain, but just barely. 'When do they plan on doing this?'

'I don't know. Soon.'

'Then where? And how many?'

London signalled to one of his guards and a rifle muzzle slowly began to rise and point at me.

'They're in the West End, down near Davie.'

The rifle drooped. London nodded for me to continue, reassured by the old place names.

'There are a couple of hundred of them and they've taken over a school. They're the ones who call themselves the Awakened. They're well-armed.' This was a lie, but the results were what I'd hoped for. Eyes that had been locked on mine now met each other around and around the room. My stock was rising. 'I can help you.'

London took his time replying and when he did his accent

was back in place. 'What makes you think you can help us, old chap? What makes you think we need your help?'

'I didn't say you needed it. I just said I could offer some assistance. If you choose to accept my offer.'

He nodded, mollified. 'And what is your offer?'

'They see me as some sort of prophet. It sounds weird, but they'll do anything I tell them to. I can keep an eye on their plans, keep you in the loop.'

'And why are you making this very kind offer?'

'It sounds like you don't want the children in the park hurt. Neither do I. That puts us on the same side.'

Dr London chewed on my words for a good long while.

I knew he wouldn't be able to fault my logic. What I didn't know, though, was why he didn't want the kids in the park killed. What did he have in mind for them? A kind of collective cognitive fog cloaked the Cat Sleepers. On some level they had to know their time was as limited as that of the people outside their chain link fences. So what was their game?

The doctor spoke. 'Do me the kindness of taking a walk around the base while I think your offer over. In fact, it's late in a busy day, and I need some sleep. We can talk more in the morning.'

'Sure.' I stood up and left the cafeteria as London gathered a couple of his people around him and they began to talk in excited whispers.

The main floor of Science World was large: ten or twenty thousand square feet of mostly open space beneath the dome.

For the next few hours, as I wandered around, London's soldiers watched me out of the corners of their eyes but kept at their tasks, which mostly appeared to consist of arranging and rearranging their formidable arsenals of weapons and food: they must have raided a Costco and a Home Depot back before things went completely apeshit. Nobody wanted to talk, but everywhere I went people stared hard at me.

A couple of dozen cots had been set up in the former gift shop near the front of the building and the windows covered by thick sheets of black felt. I could make out a few of London's people as they lay on their backs in the dark, eyes closed, faking sleep for the same reason a woman fakes an orgasm or a man professes religious conversion: desperation to belong. Probably, they thought they really were sleeping.

In the furthest corner of the main space, a curtained-off area with two sentries posted outside attracted my attention.

'What's in there?' I asked one.

'The lab,' she replied, eyes twitching as she exchanged a nervous look with her partner.

'What sort of lab?'

'The doctor's operating theatre. It's where he does his—'

'If you don't know, you shouldn't ask,' her partner butted in angrily. 'Questions lead to lies.'

I was about to ask about his curious statements, which rang with Orwellian undertones, when I saw something that made me keep my mouth shut. Just behind a gap in the curtains that served as the entrance to London's 'operating theatre' stood a cardboard box filled to overbrimming with running shoes of various sizes. Buzz Lightyear's face grinned wickedly at me from a tiny pair on top.

Then a voice from behind me: 'Dr London is ready for you now.'

Back in the cafeteria, combed and clean, London and six of his people, Dave among them, were all sitting on one side of a table, like a kind of military tribunal.

'We've decided to accept your offer,' London announced grandly. 'One of our goals for pushing west into the city will be to save the children in the park. But if these people you speak of put their evil plans into action first, it could be a disaster. So here's what will happen. We will return you to this school of yours, and in return you will keep us informed as to the group's plans. When they choose a date for invading the park, you will let us know. Can we trust you?'

'Honestly?'

'Yes.'

'You don't know if you can or not. But you have to. And I have to trust you. Isn't that right?

London scowled. 'Yes, I guess that's about right.'

He wasn't happy, and I didn't blame him. There was no way I was going to help add to the sad pile of running shoes behind that curtain. But neither of us had any choice for the moment.

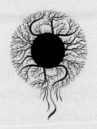

DAY 12
RAW LOBSTER

A policeman. Lobsters, before they are boiled, are a dark blue.

Next morning Dave and two other heavily-made-up Cat Sleepers escorted me back to the West End in total silence. I was pretty sure they'd been ordered not to speak to me and they were twitchy—quick to take aim at anything that moved. We took the same route as the day before: SkyTrain tracks to Granville, then a quick march down the centre of Robson to Denman, past the scene of the previous day's 'angel sighting' where a carpeting of new bodies were being feasted upon by dogs, cats, and miscellaneous birds. Dave and his companions snigger-whispered among themselves as the cats hissed and the dogs growled proprietarily.

Thank God for the ocean breeze, because the city was beginning to stink. There had always been an edge of rot to the air near the ocean, but that edge was becoming decidedly sharp as it mixed with the growing reek of Nod. But then, people who extolled the benefits of sea breezes had always ignored the decay mixed in with the salt. After all, what were seashells but empty coffins? What were starfish on the beach but bloated corpses, rotting in an alien environment?

A slight digression. For anyone with an interest in words, Lewis Carroll has always been a sort of demi-god and his Wonderland a clear precursor for Nod, with Charles as a kind of Humpty Dumpty, declaring his suzerainty over the kingdom of words. That morning, smelling the rancid tang of the air, I remembered his hate poem, "The Sea". Tonight as I write this, I can't get it out of my mind. Here's about half of it, all the stanzas, at any rate, that I can remember:

> There are certain things— a spider, a ghost,
> The income-tax, gout, an umbrella for three -
> That I hate, but the thing that I hate the most
> Is a thing they call the sea.

> Pour some salt water over the floor -
> Ugly I'm sure you'll allow it to be:
> Suppose it extended a mile or more,
> That's very like the sea.

> Beat a dog till it howls outright -
> Cruel, but all very well for a spree;
> Suppose that one did so day and night,
> That would be like the sea.

I had a vision of nursery-maids;
Tens of thousands passed by me -
All leading children with wooden spades,
And this was by the sea.

Who invented those spades of wood?
Who was it cut them out of the tree?
None, I think, but an idiot could -
Or one that loved the sea.

Isn't that Nod? That edge of cruelty and danger? Those spades cut from the trees that line Birchin Lane? Carroll, that strange bachelor, always befriending little girls on trains and writing them letters. This particular poem, I'm pretty sure, was written to just such a child. Creepy crawly. Charles, the Admiral of the Blue, was a species of nursery-maid as well as a Humpty Dumpty. I imagined him on his Rabbit Hunt, but hunting children, not leading them. An army outfitted with paddles and threshing sticks cut from the cedars of Stanley Park. Paddle-shaped wounds in all the trees.

It's late, and I'm writing by candlelight. Only a couple of tea candles left. Eight hours of light packed into each, or so their packaging claims. Down below, on the street, Charles' people are singing; they're always singing cheesy old pop songs lately.

Bye Bye, Miss American Pie
Drove my Chevy to the levy but the levy was dry...

They sing all day and night in what must be a deliberate effort to keep me awake. Sometimes I hear soft snatches of an old Beatles tune, other times frenzied takes on nursery rhymes. "Yellow Submarine" and "Twinkle, Twinkle" on endless repeat. Sometimes the sounds chill me. Other times, they make me laugh, but when that happens, the foaming-over sound of my own voice makes me realize that there's no real escape or release to be had.

Transcribing Carroll's words just now, I found myself stopping and dwelling on the word 'sea' as it appears on the page. The letters S, E, and A have lost whatever glue was holding them together, and this is like Nod as well: A S E A S E A S E A S E A S E...

We turned a corner and saw the school. Then gaped.

In my absence of less than a day, the entire building had been painted bright yellow, every last brick of it. Every door. Even most of the windows had been covered with thick splashes of the bright, sticky paint. The effect was of some art installation designed by a cynical, grant-benumbed artist to 'blow the minds' of the general public. And somehow the building also looked smaller now, like a Tonka Toy schoolhouse.

Its grounds were seething with bolstered numbers of the Awakened; Charles' Thousand was getting within reach.

'That the place?' Dave now spoke for the first time that morning and there was a sardonic edge to his voice.

'That's it.'

He grunted. 'Poor bastards. They must have raided every hardware store in the city to get enough paint for that.'

'Makes you feel kind of sorry for them,' one of the other guards said quietly.

'Almost,' Dave growled. 'Almost does. Christ, there are a lot of them.'

What must it have felt like, gazing out of one claptrap world, straight into another? The Cat Sleepers had to have seen their own reflections staring back at them at a moment like that.

Dave looked around for a while then pointed to an apartment about two blocks from the school, one with a direct sightline of the yellow monstrosity. 'We'll be setting up shop over there. Take this flashlight and when you find out when their little Rabbit Hunt is supposed to begin, flash it on and off out that window. Day or night. We'll be watching.'

He handed me a small red flashlight and pointed to a window on the top floor of the southeast corner of the school, the only one on that side of the building that remained unpainted.

'Got it?'

I nodded and put the flashlight in my pocket.

'Good. Now, when you've done that, make your way to the alley behind the school and wait. We'll meet you there and take you away from this fucking nuthouse.'

Then they left me. Dave had said 'nuthouse', but he'd been staring at the school like a covetous squirrel.

As I drew near, a few of the people on the lawn came running to greet me, giving my return a deranged 'daddy's home' vibe. The excited reception was something of a relief as I'd considered it a toss up as to whether they'd greet or eat me following my recent disappearance.

The first to speak was a pale young guy I vaguely remembered as having been up front during my speech on the lawn. He had the tangled hair and wide, unblinking eyes of a true believer— all dilated, receptive pupil. True Believers always look, to me, like dogs with their heads out the car window: in the grip of something they can't comprehend but surrendering to the joy of it without thought or reservation. A pretty picture until you reach over and surprise it with a pat on the back.

'Oh, hey. Hi. You're back! Where were you?' He kept asking questions as his companions gathered around me. 'What did you see? Why did you leave?' Apparently, I was the grain of sand in the oyster of Nod and some sort of pearl of wisdom was expected. Have you seen the ship, Paul?'

He said my name shyly, as though aware of some presumption, then stopped, having stumbled, through trial and error, upon the zeitgeist of the hour: the mysterious new arrival in English Bay. The crowd was now packed tight around me, and the stench made me want to gag. There was no chance of escape, but then again I didn't want to escape. There was nowhere on earth left to go but forward, toward Zoe and what remained of Tanya somewhere inside that sick-yellow school.

'As a matter of fact,' I lied, 'I was just on the ship.'

A circle of gasps: there wasn't a doubter among them.

'Want to know what I saw there?'

They didn't reply. Didn't even breathe, just held their gasps in their chests and waited.

'People who have a message for us, and they've come all across the ocean from China to deliver it.'

Women and men began to weep. A dozen voices asked the same question at the same time. 'What message? Are they Awake like us? Are they here to help us?'

I raised my hands. 'I'll tell you when the time comes, but right now I have a message I need to give to the Admiral.'

I pushed and the crowd yielded. The main doors were flung open, and I marched inside. Fuck Charles. I was going to grab Tanya and Zoe and make a break for it. Fuck London and his Cat Sleepers too.

The school's interior had been painted the same yellow as its exterior and the smell was almost overwhelming. The floor was tacky with paint, and walking those halls was like passing through the sickly intestines of some giant cartoon whale. I went straight upstairs to the classroom where I'd left Zoe, trailed by a dribbling of the mob from outside.

The door to the classroom was open, and Zoe was gone. The classroom itself remained unpainted, just as I'd left it. Sat in the middle of the floor, like a parent waiting up for a partying teen, sat the nameless grizzly.

'Where's Char…the Admiral?' I demanded of the wild-haired young man.

'He's in the Blue Room. Down there.'

The Blue Room. If anything had been funny anymore, that would have been hilarious. I envisioned Charles on a blue throne, listening to some demented modern jazz quartet, snapping his fingers while snacking on blue cheese.

'Show me the way.'

We all marched down the hall past doddering, shadowy forms to the Blue Room. I pushed open the door and went inside.

There was something bathetic in the plain fact of the room's blueness, and I laughed out loud at the sight. In many ways, Charles was still the Charles I had known before: sad and silly. The room was filled with a bizarre assemblage of looted goods: expensive-looking paintings and hangings; shelves of hardcover books; the biggest flat screen television I'd ever seen; and a hundred pieces of bric-a-brac piled in the corners. In the centre of this bizarre bazaar sat Charles, of course, sprawled on a royal blue sofa and ready for his audience with me.

And Tanya. She was sitting on his lap, nuzzling his pimply neck. The sight made my breath catch in my throat, but I couldn't say it was unexpected. Why wouldn't Charles have made this happen? Why wouldn't he have taken even this from me?

Tanya stared straight ahead, through me, through the wall, toward some distant place I couldn't see. A thin white dressing gown covered her body. She was shaking and coughing, not bothering to cover her mouth.

Charles started talking the instant he saw me. 'It's really true, isn't it? What they say in the New Testament? That a prophet gets no honour in his hometown? That he can't do miracles on his home turf? Can't get it up, spiritually? Would you say that you're in concurrence, Paul?'

The 'Admiral' had always made it cringingly obvious that he'd read a lot of books. He'd been a regular at the Joe Fortes library before, but probably shouldn't have bothered. Books hadn't brought him closer to people, they'd dragged him farther away. Seeing Tanya here with him, it occurred to me that whatever she had once seen in me, she probably now saw—in a funhouse mirror way—in Charles. It was a hard thought to accommodate.

I swallowed and tried not to look at Tanya. 'What have you done with the little girl?'

He ignored me. 'I always wondered about Jesus, you know. What do you think it meant when he couldn't do his miracles for the folks back home in Galilee? Know what I think? I think maybe that detail is a tiny little truth that snuck into the narrative and survived a couple of thousand years. Maybe there were no miracles. Maybe Jesus was a faker and the folks back home just didn't fall for his bullshit. Fucking prophets. What do you think, Paul?'

I thought fast. 'Why a faker? Maybe there's another explanation. What if he never pretended to be the Son of God? Maybe all that talk of miracles is just a bunch of bullshit that desperate little toadies made up hoping to keep their fingers stuck in the magical pie after they killed him.'

Charles' grin dropped dead. 'Fuck you, Paul.'

'Where's the kid? We had a deal.'

'Demon, Paul! Demon. Look at it from our perspective.

We didn't know if you were coming back. We had to put it somewhere safe. It might have bitten someone. Did you all know that Paul here keeps demons as pets?'

Murmurs from the massed flesh behind me.

'I have my reasons for the things I do. I wrote the book on this place, Admiral. Or have you forgotten that? You got all of this,' I swept my hand around the room and included Tanya, 'from me. What I choose to do with 'demons' is my own business. Where is she?'

By way of response, Charles stared at me while slipping his hand inside Tanya's robe and caressing her stomach. The fabric slipped and parted, revealing concave shadow and bone white light. She continued to stare straight ahead as though nothing was happening. My own reaction was to feel the blood in my veins freeze. I knew that if I lost my cool in front of the Awakened, they'd turn on me in a heartbeat.

'I'll give the demon to you soon enough, Paul. In the meantime, though, there's another playmate of yours here that you might be glad to see.'

With his free hand, he pointed toward my left. There in the corner a body hung from the ceiling upside down like something from a Tarot deck. A long cotton rope had been coiled around and around its legs, mummifying them. Captain America's red white and blue were barely discernible through the mess. But the truly terrible thing was what had been done to Brandon's head; it had been submerged in a bucket of the same bright yellow paint that had been used on the building. Thick drops splattered on the blue floor around the can whispered of struggle, of the agonies of drowning.

'We found him where you left him, fast asleep. He wouldn't wake up no matter how we shook him. All that work we put into his redemption wasted.'

'Fucking Sleeper piece of shit,' a voice behind me whispered.

Charles' hand was now on Tanya's now-exposed breast and was pulling and pinching at the nipple.

'Say 'hi' to Paul, Medusa,' Charles instructed her.

She swallowed, then glanced at me and grinned like some blissed-out hippie chick. 'Hey, Paul. What's up?'

I didn't answer, just tried to keep from puking, or from walking over and throttling Charles.

'Paul, do you want this to be a public meeting or a private one?'

I choked the words out. 'Private.'

'Everybody out!'

The people behind me jerked backwards, and the door closed behind them. Charles sighed.

'Alone at last. Now here's the deal, Paul. You're going to play prophet for a few more days and then you're going to anoint me—don't laugh—King of Nod.'

I didn't take his advice. In fact, I laughed immoderately. My immediate thought was to compare Charles' proclamation to the very Noddish Michael Jackson and his bizarre self-coronation as the 'King of Pop' back when the singer's personal disintegration was accelerating so quickly (as quickly as Tanya's or Charles', almost) that only a Big Lie in the form of a phrase like that could even pretend to do damage control. But then Jackson died, and people started calling him the King of Pop 'for real'. And by the time the world ended, the uncomfortable facts of the singer's life seemed to have been completely expunged from the popular narrative. So I had no doubt Charles could make his coronation stick, could glue that thorny crown to his feverish red pate.

Scowling, he took his hand off Tanya's breast and placed it behind her head. He pushed sharply down; she tumbled to her knees and began to fumble with the zipper of his pants.

'Get to work, Medusa.'

Tanya took out his flaccid penis and began to suck on it. I looked away, but there was no place for my eyes to rest.

Nothing new here. Sex had been trying to go public for a long time before Nod was spawned. Public and corporate: a pubic IPO. All that porn. Wade in deep enough and you'd see someone you knew down there: your neighbour, your teacher, your sister, your wife—writhing on the screen in some grimacing parody of ecstasy—ecstasy itself a ghost, long since vanished from the scene.

'Stop it, Charles. Stop it now.' The coldness of my voice shocked me even more than the sight I was witnessing. I was now someplace cold, someplace beyond emotion. I could kill or die, it made no difference to me. But what Charles was doing amounted, in my book, to the desecration of a corpse, and I wasn't going to let it continue.

'We're at an impasse, Paul. How about that?' He slapped the spine of the couch with the palms of both his outstretched hands while Tanya's head bobbed mechanically below. 'We appear to have reached a fucking impasse.' He grunted with pleasure, but his penis wasn't erect. 'Fucking is done for us, Paul. In case you're interested. For Medusa, this is mostly just a form of meditation and hygiene. My hygiene. When you're Awake like we are, you turn away from fantasy. Your pretend world of sleep, your games of love and fucking. It's pathetic.'

I began to move toward him, but he hurriedly pushed Tanya away.

'That's enough! Slow down, Paul. Think about the child. You don't want your precious Zoe to get hurt!"

That stopped me. I stood there as Charles zipped himself up and Tanya rose and fastened her robe. Again she coughed. Shivered. Stared straight ahead.

Charles was talking fast, trying to normalize things again. 'I need another day or two to get ready for the Rabbit Hunt, Paul. There's no reason why we can't both have what we want. What do you say?'

I felt close to tears. 'They're just kids. Why do you want to hurt them?'

He sighed patiently. 'It's not about hurting anyone, Paul. It's about sleep. Your buddy sleep was never any friend of mine. Believe me, after a day wandering the alleys and with night coming on cold and no bed on the horizon, sleep was never something I looked forward to. While you were snoozing the night away up there in the sky, I was down there in the dark, Paul, with my eyes wide open. That was my kingdom, even though I never asked for it. But it prepared me for Nod. And in Nod no one gets away with sleeping. Not on my watch.'

'What if I call in those people out there in the hall and tell them *you're* a demon?'

'Feel free to try. Right now they accept you as a mystery. A freak. They might believe you, but then again, they might believe almost anything either of us say. If our mythologies start to clash, I'd say it's a toss up as to which of us will still have all our arms and legs attached five minutes from now. And don't forget the example of poor Sleepy Headed William,' he nodded toward Brandon's body. 'It wouldn't take much for them to turn against you. And then there's your little demon, of course. What are you doing with it in that room of yours, Paul? Fucking it? I bet you still like to fuck. Right?'

At this, Tanya's white face flushed and she bit her lip until a thin line of blood dribbled down her chin like jelly from a doughnut. There was still someone inside her body, then, some vestige of her soul huddled in a dark corner of that ravaged mind.

'One more speech. One more and then you give me the child and let us go.'

'One more speech, and you anoint me king. Then you can go.'

'Fine.'

I knew that this was bullshit, of course. There would be no delivery of Zoe once I 'anointed' Charles. By agreeing, all I was doing, at best, was buying myself two or three days. He knew it too.

'A gentlemen's agreement. So glad we're past our impasse.' He was taking on what he saw as courtly tones now. 'As a way of putting our differences in the past, can I offer you a free ride on Medusa? It won't mean much to her, but it might mean something to you. No? Then get out of here.'

These last words were addressed to Tanya, who stumbled past me out the door, head down. We were alone now, except for Brandon's body.

'Charles.'

'Yes?'

'Do you believe in any of this? In Nod?'

'Who's asking? Hello? Who's asking, please?'

Without an audience, Charles seemed to shrivel. I wondered how much of an effort it took for him to hold Nod together in his unravelling mind. He was no better off than Tanya, really.

'I'm asking. Paul. You know all this Nod stuff is bullshit and that the reality is you're dying, that you'll be just another corpse in the street a week or so from now. And that you're insane.'

But Charles wasn't listening. He seemed to have forgotten I was in the room. He drifted over to the window and was whispering to himself, his fingers dragging down the glass.

'Fly, fly, little birdie. Fly, fly. I am a Child of Nodgod. A babe in the imperial woods…'

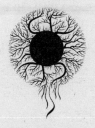

DAY 13
ABRAHAM'S BOSOM

The repose of the happy in death.

Whatever final sleep had come for Brandon was coming for me as well—and maybe even faster than death was barrelling toward the Awakened. But I had one or two things left to accomplish in Nod before I allowed myself that release. And so when I got back to the classroom I made myself a jabbing nest of old math textbooks in hopes that I'd be able to sleep on a razor's edge—exhausted enough to doze, but uncomfortable enough that I wouldn't drift too far from the shores of Nod.

It worked, and I managed to contort my way through another night, and just as Ebeneezer Scrooge famously wondered if his ghostly visitations were poorly-digested morsels of cheese, so too was my return to consciousness a stiff piece of *Math Fundamentals 6* jutting into my ribcage.

That night my dream was somewhat different. I was a five-hundred-foot tall giant striding through Vancouver, carelessly toppling skyscrapers with my elbows. There were people on the streets below, and I felt them burst like blueberries beneath the soles of my bare feet. For some reason I had to make it to the ocean and across the Georgia Strait to Vancouver Island where a tidal wave was about to crash on the west shore. But before I could enter the water, a massive wave broke over the ghostly sliver of the island visible on the horizon. And then, of course, the world exploded. This time, however, as the last fragments dissolved into Golden Light, I saw the park, intact. Children running through the trees, mouths contorted in either laughter or terror.

The next morning, I woke to find someone had left an unopened bag of chips on the floor for my breakfast: Zesty Cheese Doritos. I ate them as best I could, though I tasted nothing and the exercise left me with a sore gut, raw lips, and a raging thirst. I crumpled the metallic bag, and the sound was hangover loud. Then I sat on the warm linoleum by the window and thought about Tanya.

True story. One New Year's Eve a couple of years ago, she drank far, far too much, then spent the hours between midnight and dawn vomiting repeatedly, anywhere and everywhere. She puked in the same way heavy smokers clear their throats, casually, unconsciously. I spent those hours following her around with a bucket, holding her hair back, and listening to her laugh and cry, laugh and cry. She giggled about a conversation she'd had with a friend earlier that evening, then grew angry about it, then wept. Swampwatered all over the place. Shook her head fiercely whenever I tried to utter some inept words of commiseration.

'Don't talk. Just don't,' she warned every time I opened my mouth. I remember feeling as though, robbed of my words, I had nothing else to offer. Still, all in all a tender memory. If you've ever loved somebody besides yourself that won't surprise you too much.

Someone once said that we get more difficult to love with each passing year because, over time, our histories grow so tangled that newcomers can no longer bushwhack their way into the thicketed and overgrown depths of our hearts. I'd search and cite those words for you if I could. I'd really like to give proper credit for the insight because it's true: Tanya's and my intertwined histories were like varicose veins on an old man's ankles. Who could truly *know* an old man or woman, coming cold upon them in a nursing home when they're ninety-two years old? It's too late, by then. All we see are crooked shadows, faces rewritten as caricature, fully-lived lives recast as rasped anecdotes.

Looking over at the abandoned grizzly lying face down on the floor, I remembered the blood on Tanya's chin when Charles had spoken about the kids in the park. Something about the fairy tale intensity of that red trickle made me believe that whatever spark was left in her brown eyes would flare up in Zoe's defence. All of which is a roundabout way of prefacing the revelation that I found myself roaming the halls of the school that morning. Looking for Tanya.

The Awakened were growing visibly more frail, still going about their nonsensical business, but more and more slowly. Their weary eyes were tiny movie projectors, and as they stared, I felt myself covered with wobbly tattoos of light: old home movies and horror scenes. There was a lot of sneezing and coughing going on all around me as ravaged immune systems fizzled and sparked.

'Do you know where Medusa is?' I asked the first person I met, a teenaged girl wearing a full-face motorcycle helmet. She was walking down a hall, tapping on the walls every six inches then listening.

She nodded, smiling strangely.

'Where?'

But she just shook her head and recommenced tapping and listening, face pressed against the self portraits and box-and-triangle drawings of houses floating beneath a sea of yellow paint.

'I know where Medusa is.'

I turned and saw my wild-haired young friend. The believer.

'Where is she?'

'My name's White-in-the-eye.' It was once said that the devil had no white in his eye. 'I can take you there.'

He led me to the next floor down, then toward the furthest end of the hall, talking all the while.

'How did you know it was coming?'

That stumped me. *Had* I seen Nod coming? It was true that

part of me had always remained outside the old world—a ghost with folded arms. I think I always suspected that some sort of fraud was being perpetuated as I watched 'normal' play out. Maybe I just expected more of life than it was realistically even going to be able to deliver—maybe I was a romantic.

Real romantics are never the ones with the easy, winning ways about them; the real romantics are always the guarded ones, the paranoid and the worried, the ones with furrowed brows and coffee jitters. After all, anybody looking with open eyes at the world we'd made would have to have been very, very worried.

So maybe, in that way, I had seen Nod's skull and crossbones mast on the horizon.

'Maybe. Maybe I saw two worlds, one on top of the other. But it was fuzzy, like when you try on someone else's glasses.'

White-in-the-eye nodded gravely, then asked me about the ship again. Soon we stopped outside a closed door. Then he turned and spoke, tipsy with revelation.

'You dreamed up Nod when you wrote your book, right? But Nod wasn't the dream—the old world was. When you were dreaming of Nod, you were really awake! That's why you're the prophet.'

And I got it then. The Awakened had it backward. The old 'reality' of Vancouver had been unreal, a dream. Yes. I was with them that far. But the real reality wasn't Nod—Nod was just all the dreams and nightmares smushed together in a blender. *Real* reality would be whatever remained intact after Nod had hammered down upon our heads and ripped away the last shreds of the veil of the old world. And that would be? What would endure?

Tanya.

White-in-the-eye opened the door and showed me a yellow room awash with light. The sun, visible through the window, smelled like a coat of fresh paint. Tanya lay propped up against a desk, hunched forward, hands between her spread legs. She was breathing with great effort: The Little Engine That Probably Couldn't For Much Longer. Oxygenated blood wasn't reaching her gray fingertips and blackened toes. Each breath was a momentous decision, undertaken only after serious consideration. And she wasn't alone. Outside this room, Death was stalking the dusty halls, picking and choosing as he went. Out in the alley, there was a reeking, akimbo pile of meat that grew every day when I wasn't looking.

I went over and tried to ease her down onto her back, but she screamed and threw her face at me. It was a horrible sight.

'I won't lie down and you can't fucking make me!'

'But you can't breathe like this.'

'I can't lie, can't lie. Sleepers are liars! Golden light, golden lie…'

Weakly, she pushed away the hand I'd placed on her shoulder. She was someone you might have seen begging on a street corner in the Third World: too far gone for genteel Developed World beggary, for the haute couture of the Salvation Army-swathed squeegee kid. She smelled like rotten fish and vomit. I had to turn away to take a breath, and when I turned back she was coughing and gurgling to herself. Her words, though unintelligible, had the intonation of conversation.

'Tanya. I need to find Zoe. You remember Zoe? The little girl we found? You gave her that stuffed bear?'

She stopped mumbling and looked up, looked at me. Suddenly, someone was home, though peering through a filthy attic window. I struggled to hold her gaze as she crooked her finger, drew me nearer, and whispered, 'Why didn't you like people, Paul?'

How could I have replied to that? I could have confessed that I liked the idea of people, but not the reality. I could have said that in some insane way White-in-the-eye had been right and that I *had* seen Nod coming and had been hoping to stand clear of its path. Instead, I opted for the truth.

'I don't know why.'

'I'd have left you I'd have left you I'd have left you I'd…' Then she stopped and changed direction. 'What did you dream last night?'

'I was a giant, taller than the skyscrapers. Walking toward the beach. Then a tidal wave came over the horizon. The water was shining, and it really hurt my eyes.'

'What happened next?' She'd heard this story before and was suddenly playing an old game called 'story time'.

'The world exploded.'

'Like a bomb hit it?'

I shook my head into her shoulder. 'No. Not like that at all. More like it was a collage where the pieces weren't glued down and someone opened the door and all the pieces just fluttered away.'

'Just blew away…poor baby. Then what?' She was being the little girl she'd sometimes liked to be. More than once, in the past, I'd wondered if she stuck with me because I was good at recounting old fairy tales. Because I was good at bedtime stories.

'Then the pieces all disappeared and there was nothing left but golden light.'

She burrowed into me. 'And then what?"

'Just light. It went on forever.'

Tanya looked up toward my face, but her eyes could no longer see, which meant it looked as though she saw everything. This was how she would die. This was how the world was dying.

'Pretty Zoe's in the furnace room. It's hot down there. Hot as Hell's Gate…'

She smiled as she trailed off. Then another murder. I cut her throat with an orange box cutter I found in a cupboard then cradled her head, suddenly tiny and nut hard beneath all that raving hair, as her body thrashed a little, but not too much, and her blood dyed my blue jeans purple.

When it was over, her earlobes, the ones she'd told me marked her as alien, marked her as mine. I bowed my head and kissed each one in turn.

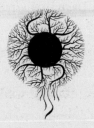

DAY 14
WALKING GENTLEMAN

In theatrical parlance, means one who has little or
nothing to say, but is expected to deport himself
as a gentleman when before the lights.

Your indulgence for an elegy.

We met in university, in a second year philosophy class. I was there because I believed that three hundred year old arguments about the nature of the universe were somehow time sensitive (I know, I know), while Tanya enrolled—so she said—because the class fit her timetable. After we graduated I went on to write my books and she became a well-paid publicist for a fairly large chemical company with a host of dubious contracts. We strove to maintain the fine balance I mentioned earlier, with intellectual 'purity' on my side of the ledger and the slapping heft of the bacon she brought home on Tanya's. When the pedal hit the metal and the rubber hit the road, though, the scales tipped in her favour. She could mock my financial worthlessness all she wanted, but I couldn't really dig too deeply at her hollow careerism given that it put bread on the corporeal table. Rather than confront this disconnect in some conclusive manner, however, we did as most couples and just lived with it as best we could.

Ours was a classic mismatch with all the makings of a screwball comedy. Did hilarity ensue? Sometimes. At other times, though, during the outtakes, awkward silences and buried resentments ensued as well. And if you made a two-hour movie covering a seven year relationship there were going to be a *lot* of outtakes. But still, we soldiered on.

After three or four years together, we began to understand one another a little. It came to light that Tanya liked my verbosity because it spoke to something trapped inside her that needed to get out. As for me, there was something appealing about the outward shell she'd been developing, her World Armour. The hardness of that shell implied a softness at the centre, a secret place into which I probably hoped I could retreat—a mirror for my own lack of outward form—when I got sick of the sound of my own voice or the thought balloon shape of my own thoughts.

Then, as time loped along, Tanya changed in a way I could never quite get my head around. Maybe her armour thickened to the point where there was no point of entry for someone as amorphous as me. Amorphous: that's amore, always morphing. It got tricky when I realized one day that I'd have to begin to get used to the idea of living without the shelter she'd once seemed to offer, and that she'd have to accept that I was needy. But still we kept trudging forward. Maybe everyone had to wade through this muck, we thought. Still, there was now something stranger-like about her; and I sensed that if we were to remain together, I'd have to learn to love and protect that strangeness.

It sounds like a bleak landscape, but it wasn't, not really. There were romantic sunsets and soft shadows as well as forensic facts under antiseptic light. We made love and laughed together. And we watched our favourite shows throughout what had to be the Golden Age of Television, no matter how dubious a sobriquet that is. We liked to cook together on Sunday afternoons. Those things counted too.

At least that's how I saw it. God knows I never said any of this stuff, not to Tanya or to anybody else. Nobody *says* these things— it's against the rules—but deep inside we know that we are, each of us, unknowable and ultimately alone, even when we love.

Most of the people we'd known were busy playing out a game of 'no limits' in their relationships and careers. They were serial Humpty Dumpties, falling apart then putting themselves back together again, over and over, beneath new horizons made of unfamiliar hips and thighs. Maybe I'd been unsociable because I feared infection, and maybe Tanya had been out there with them, swimming around in the genetic soup. I'd thought Tanya and I were different, that we were going to swallow reality whole and let it live inside us despite the surfeit of fantasy on offer. Big oops: in the end it turned out that reality was bigger and crueller than I'd imagined.

Wherever my love for Tanya lived, wherever it lives now, that place was neither the old Vancouver nor Charles' cracked-out Fantasyland. Love lives someplace else. Is that it? Or are there simply no words for what I'm trying to say?

In the basement a skeletal crew. Eyes bulging in the dimness, they sat hunched over tables strewn with rusty iron bars, steel hooks, baling wire, and rope. Working, making. Long staves with ragged clusters of sharp metal fixed to their ends. Floating above candles, their faces were goblin-like. All around them, in the dimness, a forest of completed staffs were stacked against the walls. The weapons appeared numberless, but I knew how many there were, or would very soon be: precisely a thousand.

A gate to Hell? Yes.

But was Zoe down here? I peered hard into the dim and distant corners. There didn't seem to be anywhere to hide her, but then again the basement was a cavernous place—a moonscape of unfinished concrete and impenetrable shadows. It was terrible to think of that poor little thing, so obviously a creature that belonged in the light, locked away down there.

Then I saw it—the school's ancient furnace skulking, cold and dunce-like in a far corner; a rusted box with an arthritic assemblage of pipes extending up into the rafters. A small iron door in its exact centre. If you lived in a place like Nod, where else would you stow a demon?

The goblins were beginning to notice my presence. Several were watching me, eyes probing but not penetrating, jaws working silently.

'What? What?' asked a woman at the nearest table. 'What?'

'Will you be ready soon?' I asked as imperiously as I could manage. It's tough work being a prophet: every time you ask someone for the time, your reputation is in mortal peril.

She nodded for a full ten seconds, eyes shut, before replying. 'Yes, yes, we'll be ready when the sun comes up. Not the next sun, but the one after. Yes, yes. We're almost ready…'

In two days, then. It was time to give the Cat Sleepers their heads up.

It was almost dawn. Back in the classroom, I signalled Dave as instructed. Almost as soon as I'd finished, an answering flash came from down the block. If nothing else, insomniacs make great watchmen. I ran down to the black alley, exchanged a few whispered words with the three Cat sleepers, then crept back upstairs and turned my mind back to Zoe. If the Rabbit Hunt was to take place in two days, then tomorrow would be the obvious time to rescue her from the basement, given that almost all of Charles' people would be otherwise occupied. It wasn't an airtight plan—it wasn't a plan at all—but it was a hope. And a hope in Nod was *something*.

My eyes were burning and raw, and I wanted nothing more than to lie down on my bed of textbooks and close them for a while. But before I could move, rough hands grabbed me from behind, and Charles's voice whispered into my ear.

'No biggie, Paul, no biggie. Nobody's going to hurt you, but there's something down at the beach that you really need to see.'

That 'something' was colossal. An aircraft carrier, run aground on the edge of English Bay. The American warship— the name '*USS Nassau*' was painted on its side—appeared to have approached land under full power and had managed to beach itself so far up onto the shore that the prow was completely exposed. Five or six storeys high, one side of its grey hull was blackened and pitted, torn and buckled, while the other side was untouched—unflinching grey in the early morning sunlight. The crowning bizarreness to the scene was the sound coming from within the vessel: humming, low and steady, but with shrill overtones that wove in and out. Someone had neglected to turn off the engine. Clearly, this was the ship whose lights I'd seen out in the bay.

Beside me, Charles stared hard, trying to cram the sight into Nod. He looked like shit—like one of those inflated dummies you'd see outside drive-thru espresso kiosks, the ones that, powered by a big fan, would fill with air, trembling and rigid, then go limp for a moment only to inflate again seconds later. On the way over here, he'd limped when he walked and drooled when he talked, wiping his nose constantly.

We'd arrived here at the head of a silent procession of around two hundred of the Awakened. They now stood arrayed around us in a protective ring, and that was a good thing, because we were far from alone on that beach. Around the ship, around us, hundreds of others were gathered. Charles' contingent, which had felt mighty when we'd left the yellow school, now seemed decidedly puny.

It suddenly struck me that not everyone left alive even knew about Nod. Everyone? *Holy shit*, I thought, almost no one knew about Nod. The vast majority of the Awakened were living in nameless kingdoms of their own terrified devising, and now they were ranged all around us, trembling and grinding their teeth. The creatures I'd seen two nights ago had now taken human forms, but were no less bizarre for that.

'What do you think, Paul?' Charles asked in a conversational tone. He'd pulled himself together: there was no indication in his ruby red eyes that he was impressed by the immensity of what we were all gawking at—or that he'd heard of Tanya's death.

'You're the Admiral of the Blue. You tell me.'

He didn't answer, so I looked around. The crowd appeared weak and disoriented, dangerous only in the heft of their numbers, though that was dangerous enough. How did they keep going? They must have been reduced to drinking drain water and licking empty tins of cat food clean by now. Walking back from the SkyTrain station I'd seen a group of women gnawing bark peeled from an arbutus tree, red like beef jerky. Swallow. Cramp. Retch. Repeat.

Suddenly, Charles spoke loudly, to everyone within earshot.

'We'll board the ship! Your Admiral will greet its captain! Make room!'

A cheer from the residents of Nod at this and a curious craning of necks from the rest. Charles's eyes were glazed with fierce tears as he watched his people clear a spot on the beach near the ship, into which we quickly moved. I almost felt happy for the poor bastard; you couldn't deny that he'd come a long way from cadging conversational scraps along Denman Street.

Hands on hips, Charles ordered one of his men to throw a rope with a large hook tied to one end up at the destroyer's rails. No small feat, given that the ship's deck was easily forty feet above our heads and backlit by the sun to boot. It took eight or nine tries, but finally the hook cleared the rails and clanked onto the deck. The non-Nod crowd cheered this achievement and pressed forward, drawn to any display of resourcefulness and order. The Awakened's ring of linked arms, five deep, rippled but held.

'Listen!' Charles cried.

And the crowd listened.

'This ship is named the Ragnarok! There's a message for us up there on its decks, and it's a message that you all need to hear! I promise you that if you wait, you'll all hear it!'

Ragnarok. A pretty good name for a nuclear powered warship, I had to admit: the Norse word for 'apocalypse'. Better than 'Nassau' with its connotations of frat boy vacations and disco music, anyway.

The guy who'd hooked the rope somehow managed to shimmy up and disappeared over the railing. A few minutes of silence followed during which all eyes remained fixed on the ship's horizon. Finally, the black speck of the climber's head reappeared and the crowd exhaled as a rope ladder tumbled down. Charles called three of his people over. Big men and all of them had bandages around their heads, blood in caked rivulets down their necks. He pointed at the ladder, and the five of us began to climb.

* * *

The deck was echo empty. No planes, nothing except for the unbelievable complexity of the bridge tower and its cacophony of antennae and satellite dishes. A metal planet, silent except for a string of flags that snapped in the wind and the seagulls' distant, wind-borne desolation. One of Charles' damaged gym apes reached over the rail and hauled up the ladder. Now we were alone.

Charles eyed the bridge tower with the eyes of an eleven-year-old boy, longing to climb it and make it his own.

'There are worse places to die,' he mused, to himself but with my overhearing him very clearly in mind.

'Pardon?'

'Than here. In the sun. You won't mind, will you? I'd say, given recent bereavements, that you're about done with Nod. Am I wrong, Paul? It's time. Probably, it will be like one of those dreams of yours. You can lie on your back and stare at the sun while we do it. You know, Aztec-style.'

Then he nodded, and before I could react his men moved in close. I felt something cold and sharp digging into my ribs.

'A giant Roc is going to fly straight down out of the sun and martyr you, Paul. But don't worry: it's a noble ending. You'll fight back very bravely and you won't have died for nothing. You'll save my life, and as you lie dying you'll anoint me king with your last gasp—I'll make sure everyone knows you were a hero.'

I must have smirked, because Charles grew livid.

'That's how the story crumbles, Paul. All the way back from the Old Testament, the new one, and all the way through Nod:

the prophet brings the truth, and then he dies. Simple.'

I didn't answer, so he kept on talking.

'So nice that it's just you and me here at the end, Paul. They,' he indicated his crew, 'can't hear a thing, so we can talk frankly and openly. Look at that one. He was a fucking lawyer two weeks ago. That's why I chose him for my special guard: irony. He drove an Audi. Now he snips his ears off with garden shears just because I suggest that it might be a good idea if he wanted to avoid having demons whisper terrible suggestions to him in the dark. It's a wonderful world, Paul. Fucked up as it ever was, for sure, but still wonderful. A real meritocracy. Finally.'

'You can kill me if you want to, but you're going to die yourself, Charles. Really soon—you know that, right? And your Rabbit Hunt is going to fail. There's no point in any of it.'

He shook his head and spat. 'No! I've got babies in my eyes. There are babes in the wood, Paul. In Demon Park. People in the stocks, locked in the wood. Then there's babies in the eyes and that's love. So we'll have a Rabbit Hunt and we'll flush out those demons and we'll put them in the stocks and we'll have their eyes and our love will keep us alive.' He hacked desperately into his sleeve. 'You wouldn't understand. A riddle has been set, Paul. Your entire fucking manuscript is a giant riddle, and I'm the one who's solved it. Not you. You don't even know where the question marks go. The answer to the riddle is 'name it and it's yours'. And I'm—'

Charles' supervillain soliloquy was interrupted by a male voice, crackling at top volume over the ship's PA system.

'It was me! I did it!'

Charles looked around wildly. So did his crew, in earless imitation of their master. There was no way to tell where the transmission was coming from.

'It was me! If you're looking for the man, I'm the goddamned man!'

Then I saw it: movement on the bridge tower. I bolted. It took Charles and company a couple of heartbeats to react, but by then it was no contest. Charles and his goons were the walking wounded, but I was still a rough approximation of my old ten-kilometres-four-days-a-week self. By the time I reached the base of the bridge tower, they were more than fifty feet behind me.

A series of metal stairs zigzagged up the bridge's side. Picking one at random, I began to climb. I quickly learned that military ships were specifically designed to be scalable: where one set of steps ended, either another would begin or there would be a set of metal hoops welded onto the wall that led to a ladder or another set of stairs. It felt like a series of lucky breaks but my progress was really the design of whatever Norse god had constructed the Ragnarok. In no time, I was nearing the top— the winner in a giant game of Snakes and Ladders.

Meanwhile, that frantic voice was still broadcasting.

'I had a cancer brain and it told me to make a mushroom cloud. Get it? You fucking maniacs! Now I'll tell you how to make your own goddamn mushroom cloud!'

A male voice with a Texan accent whose cadence seemed to reflect the unseen speaker's military profession: driving points home in a staccato style.

'I see you coming. I see you climbing. Better come quick, boy.' His voice mocked me. 'Time's a wasting! Come on, boy! You're almost there!'

And then I was there. Standing on a thin deck that ran around the top of the bridge. I looked down. Charles and company were huffing and puffing up toward my perch. I turned and peered in through the window.

He was terribly burned. A stained officer's uniform over barbequed skin that was hanging from his body in curling chunks. And between those chunks was the molten lava of raw, red under-flesh. Scraps of hair clung to his head and his eyes were haunted blue, their whites blazing as he stared at me from across a frontier of unimaginable pain.

Tearing my eyes away, I tried to turn the door handle but it was locked. I pounded on the glass, but it wasn't glass—it was something much stronger.

'Not so fast! No one gave you permission to enter the bridge, son!'

'Let me in!'

He tapped his ear and shook his head, laughing silently, a microphone pressed between the stubs of his ruined hands.

'Your friends down there want to do you harm, do they? Worried you might get hurt? You've come to the wrong place. Son, I've killed millions. It's not that big a deal. I'm the biggest mass murderer in the history of the god damn world.'

I was listening to a public address system while, right in front of me, the officer's frayed lips synched badly to the bullhorn sound. Behind me the stairs clanged louder and louder. I looked around, but there was no other way down. Then I turned back to the officer and noticed something. His eyes. They were clear and steady amid the smoking wreckage of his face.

'Look at my eyes!' I yelled.

'What's that?'

'My eyes! I sleep. Just like you. Look at my eyes. I'm not like them.'

He staggered forward until he was a foot away, only a thin sheet of super-glass between us. It was all I could do to hold his gaze.

'Son of a bitch,' he murmured and wordlessly reached over and unlocked the door. I slipped inside and slammed it shut just as the bandaged head of one of Charles' men came into view. Within moments all three of them were pounding on the bridge's door and windows, but to no avail. I felt like sticking my tongue out at them. In fact, if I'm to be honest, I *did* stick my tongue out at them in a moment of adrenaline-fuelled triumph that only added to Charles' rage.

My host reeled backward, groping for a chair, then fell into it, wincing.

'Son of a bitch,' he repeated. 'I thought I was the only one left.'

Scattered all around the bridge, covering virtually every horizontal surface, were empty syringes.

'There aren't many of us. I've only met one other Sleeper myself. Except for the kids.

'Kids?'

'There are children in Stanley Park over there,' I gestured toward the tree line. 'They sleep. They look normal, like kids from before. But they don't talk.'

'All the kids?' His eyes shone.

'No. Not all. Most of them are like those guys out there. In fact, I think the kids who can't sleep are already all dead. They wouldn't survive for long out there. But in the park there are a few hundred of these other kids.'

'Bullshit.'

He was getting agitated again, grinding his teeth. Noticing the revolver strapped to his hip, I decided not to press the point any further. After a moment, he looked up at me, something cagey in his eyes.

'There's something I've got to tell you, man. Shit, I've got to tell someone.'

'What?'

'It was me.'

'What was you?' I asked, though the answer flashed through my mind even as I spoke.

'I took out Seattle.'

'You launched the missile?'

'Not me, exactly. But it happened on my watch and I was the only one in my right mind, so it was my fault. I was locked in my quarters, sleeping, when the others did it. But I was in command.' He said this with a kind of tortured pride, the kind I'd never been able to relate to but had the sense to respect: doctor pride, cop pride, mother pride.

'Why'd they—?'

'It was so fucking crazy and every day it got crazier and crazier. A couple of days after the whole thing started, we started having to throw men in the brig if we were going to maintain discipline. Two days later, we ran out of cells to put them in. All sorts of stories started flying around, spooking everyone. Then we had to start shooting them to keep them in line. Control told us the same thing was happening everywhere. Some of the officers rallied around me. They thought I could figure out a solution because I could think clearer. Because I could sleep. But they didn't really trust me, you know? Yeah, I can tell you know. Anyhow, they launched the fucking missile from one mile out, aimed it straight at the downtown core, at the goddamn Space Needle for all I know. Everyone on deck was killed. I survived the blast because I was sleeping down below. Fuck. The others who survived told me about some plague, how one of them had had a vision of some plague, and they had to sterilize the city to stop it. Bat shit crazy. Then they took over from me and decided to sail up here to repeat the trick. But by then I'd disabled the missile control panels and they couldn't launch. Meanwhile, we were all getting sicker and sicker from the radiation.'

'And then what?'

'And then a couple of nights ago, I took my revolver and finished off the last dozen of them. Bam, bam, bam. Like target practice. They were all just about done for anyway. It's just me now.'

'So why did you…?'

'Ram the shore?' He moistened ruined lips with a swollen tongue. 'After a few hours out there watching the shit going down on this beach I figured I might as well finish the job my men started. Not for crazy reasons, you know, but a mercy killing. Only I couldn't re-arm the nukes. You need two people with the right codes pressing the same buttons at the same times. So I thought about the reactor that runs the engines.'

'But I just told you, you're not the only sane one left. There are—'

'There's nothing left. I can't even sleep any more myself, man. It hurts so bad. I think I'm turning into one of them. I keep thinking bad thoughts. I just want to sleep. To dream. Damn, it hurts. I'll tell you one thing: now I know how a goddamned burnt hot dog feels.'

I choked up a little at that. A joke. The first one I'd heard, I was pretty sure, since this whole mess started. Humour had been the first casualty in Nod, and a humourless world seemed somehow even more tragic than one filled with pain and suffering. There has always been suffering, but humour had helped make it bearable.

He was speaking again.

'What's your name?'

'Paul.'

'Tyler. Tyler Brown. Lieutenant first class. I was.'

He shifted stiffly in his chair and winced. A pink tear started to stumble down his cracked cheek.

'Is there anything I can do for you, Tyler?'

He laughed and shook his head. 'You can shoot me, brother. You willing to do that?'

'You've got to be in a lot of pain.'

'No, man. No, I'm cruising through junkie heaven. There's twenty gallons of morphine down below.' He gestured around the room at the syringes. 'I don't feel much except when I pass by a mirror. That hurts a shitload, believe me.'

We both laughed, but it felt like a wake for laughter. Whatever their other virtues, I couldn't see the kids in the park trading quips or cracking wise.

Tyler picked up an empty syringe and threw it on the floor. 'It's a joke in so many ways, man. I joined the navy because every kid in my neighbourhood was getting hooked on shit like this. And here I'm going to end my days as a junkie.' He switched tracks. 'You hungry? There's a restaurant down below, you know. Massive chow.'

By now, the kicking and pounding had stopped. I turned and found Charles staring straight at me. There were wolves in those bloodshot eyes and a gnawing of bones in that grinding jaw. I noted that one of his henchmen was missing, probably sent to get reinforcements.

I moved close to the glass and winked at him, disappointing myself with my casual cruelty. Charles was on the outside yet again and that had to be unspeakably hard to take—especially for a newly-anointed king.

Down in the mess hall, I stuffed my face with fried bacon, canned ravioli, and that perennial military favourite, Spam. Tyler had assured me that the ship was locked down and that no one was going to be able to break in with anything less than a blowtorch and a working set of Jaws of Life.

We'd been down there for a couple of hours, trading stories

in between his morphine injections. I was becoming aware of a pattern: Tyler would get more and more agitated and angry, then inject himself and calm down for ten or twenty minutes, dreamy but lucid. He'd taken to jabbing the needle into his forearm without much of an effort to find a viable vein. There was no way he could carry on like this for much longer. What if he overdosed and died tonight? Then there would be no way to shut the ship down.

He watched me eat with what looked like envy, but took nothing for himself. Instead he sat opposite me, propped in a chair, arms stiff at his sides, taking occasional noisy sips from a juice box. It was hard to imagine how he blinked, let alone walked or sat: he seemed to be melting before my eyes. In fact, he probably was.

'How long until the reactor melts down if you don't turn it off?'

He cleared his throat. 'No idea. As it turns out, I never blew up a nuclear powered aircraft carrier before. Not too long.'

'And are you going to shut it down?'

He was ready for my question and belligerent in his reply. 'Why would I? I'll be doing us all a favour by speeding the goddamn process up by a few days. You and I get to waltz off into our dreams. And those poor bastards out there will be better off as well.' He snorted. 'Pacification of the local populace.'

'Even if you're right about that, what about the children I told you about in the park? They don't need to die.'

He was already prepping himself for another needle, the

third since I'd met him. He pushed the plunger down and fell back in his chair, needle dangling.

'It's bullshit,' he said dreamily. 'Pure, unadulterated bullshit. There's nothing left to save. I've been watching this place through my fucking high powered military fucking telescope. It's a nightmare. Pacification of the captain, pacification of the enemy. We all just want some peace. Well, I'm the goddamn peacemaker...'

His voice drifted off and I became aware of a distant, hollow pounding—Charles' people trying to smash their way inside. At dusk, we'd watched them building a bonfire on the main deck. About three dozen of the Awakened armed with crowbars and sledgehammers.

'But why not just let things play out? What if you play God and you're wrong?'

This woke him up. 'God? Don't start with God, son. If there was a God, we wouldn't be in this fucking mess. I had kids you know. Three. Amy, Jimmy, and baby Anna. They're dead. Wife dead, dog dead. Cat, too. Though I never thought much of that cat.' Here he laughed until a coughing fit cut him off. 'God? Fuck him. This, whatever's left now, it's just a shadow. The party's over, and the sooner somebody turns out the lights, the better. Am I right?'

'But the kids I'm talking about are different.'

Tyler stared straight at me with an intensity that I was beginning to find chilling. Suddenly I was aware of how alone we were down here.

'Different from my kids? Better than mine? No they fucking

aren't. Those kids of yours do sound like fucking demons. When I think about them floating around out there in the dark, not making a sound, just watching people? Honest, it sounds scarier than your buddy Charles. Christ, how those kids of yours must torment those poor sleepless bastards.'

'But—'

'Now, I'm not going to stop you from doing whatever you feel you've got to do. Just don't *you* try to stop *me* from…from…'

He fumbled around for another needle.

'Can you help me get out of the ship so I can go help that girl, Zoe I told you about?'

He reeled as the next wave of euphoria hit him, and I felt my question had at least been well-timed.

'That's nothing. There are a thousand ways out of here. You can check out any time but you can never leave…'

'What if I bring her here? Show you? Will you shut off the engines then?'

He coughed and either shook his head or shuddered as the morphine babbled through his system.

'Such a lovely place, such a lovely place…'

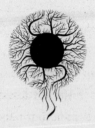

DAY 15
GOAT AND COMPASSES

A corruption of 'God en-compasses [us]'.

'You *sure* you want to go back out there?' Tyler asked dubiously, coherent for the moment.

'No, I'm not sure, but duty calls.'

I gave him a mock salute, and Tyler allowed himself a smile. It was just before dawn and we were standing on a tiny back deck, down near water level and invisible from shore at this time of day. Above us, the Ragnarok's hull rose like a cast iron skyscraper.

A little earlier, back up on the bridge, we'd watched as stooped figures on the deck, lit by lapping flames, moved back and forth. Hammering, prying, burning—looking for a weak point in the ship's armour. They'd even brought along an acetylene torch, which worried me but just made Tyler laugh contemptuously. Loud voices called back and forth. Weakened as they were, the

233

Awakened must have been finding breaking into a US aircraft carrier a very frustrating venture—something like trying to prise open a coconut with one's bare hands.

After our dinner I'd slept for six hours—the most rest I'd had in a week—in a comfortable bunk. Before going to bed I'd even showered and shaved. And now here I was, in clean clothes with a pack on my back filled with unimaginable luxuries: canned food, a knife, bottles of water. And a flare gun.

During that night's prelude to the Golden Light, I'd been—not too surprisingly—a missile flying toward some distant city, a fantastical metropolis crowded with towering spires.

Tyler had promised to wake me before sunrise and he'd come through with a series of sharp slaps to my face that finally did the trick. Then we'd made a deal. If I was able to return with Zoe, I'd shoot a flare from the beach and he'd open the back door and wait for us. I hoped that by bringing Zoe to meet Tyler I might be able to convince him to shut off the engines before they blew.

The thrumming. By now it was so loud it must have been audible all over the West End. I could only imagine the havoc it was playing on the unravelled minds of the tightly-wound denizens of Nod.

I climbed over the rail and into a dinghy that hung from a winch. Below me, the ocean churned, waves slapping against the Ragnarok's backside.

'Take care,' I said as Tyler pressed a button and the winch began to lower me down to the water.

He didn't reply, was growing distant again. He just kept his flashlight beam trained on me as I descended.

The dinghy hit the water and began to buck as I detached the winch chain and began to row toward Stanley Park. The beach around the carrier was still swarming with fire-lit shapes, but any sound they made was smothered by the noise of the Ragnarok's engines. Even though I knew no one could see me, I felt exposed. Were those figures locked in another animal bacchanal? And if so, what shape had the Ragnarok taken on in their minds?

On the other hand, the physicality of rowing and the pre-dawn dampness in the air felt terrific. Out there on the water it was as though the madness on the beach, on the ship, and in the city was all a dream. And so I row, row, rowed my boat. The same waves had rolled along these shores for millions of years; dinosaurs once bathed in the same water I now paddled through. During the intervening millennia mountains had risen and fallen and all the plants and animals had been replaced and reinvented. But the water hadn't changed.

When I finally made shore the sun was glowering on the horizon, and it was low tide. I beached the dinghy and stepped through the black, sucking mud at the water's edge toward firmer ground. The seawall, when I reached it, was only about five feet high, and I was able to clamber up onto the walkway that ran along its edge fairly easily. At my feet a stencilled man marched west toward the Lion's Gate Bridge while a stencilled cyclist headed east, back toward the Ragnarok. Deciding that both these stick creatures were nuts, I headed north—straight into the woods.

They didn't look very welcoming. Before me, titanic cedars stood aloof, with seemingly impassable thickets of blackberry bushes around their ankles. Half of Vancouver's vegetation had to be blackberry bushes and wherever forest met open sunlight, they took over. Not too far inland from where I stood, however, the woods would deepen and the underbrush thin out in the permanent shade. In fact, the park was riddled with trails; it was just a matter of finding one that would lead back downtown, and given that the park was bordered on three sides by ocean, eventually they all did. So a doable task.

I found the thinnest section of bramble I could, took a deep breath, and pushed forward. God, it hurt. Death by a thousand tiny scratches. My raised forearm protected my face, but my arms, legs, and neck were ripped and torn. Within a minute or so, however, the going got easier as cedars rose around me, their shade anathema to smaller plants. Soon I was on a well-established trail. I stopped and rubbed my arms, smearing blood everywhere, until the stinging's volume died down and I could hear the Ragnarok once more.

After I had walked for a while, there was a rustling in the brush and I spun around, fully expecting to see some demon-hunter, cudgel poised to heave ho into my skull. Instead, I saw a boy of around eleven, red-haired and freckled, thin and vulnerable-looking. Jeans and a T-shirt hung from his body like afterthoughts as he watched me with an expression of—approximately—mild interest. Perhaps it was my recent stint of stillness out in the dinghy, or perhaps it was my comparatively well-rested state, but I surprised myself. Rather than try to talk and repeat the error Tanya and I had made the first time we had encountered a group of these children, I simply sat down on the hard-packed earth in the centre of the trail and waited. The boy seemed pleased, as though I'd done exactly what he'd hoped, and immediately sat down opposite me. I felt the familiar puppet pull toward speech but forced myself to ignore it.

During the silent powwow that ensued, the sun rose above us and the world coloured itself in, a little blurry and not quite between the lines. No golden light, just a daydream moment like when we stare at a tree out the window or the lines on our hands and they become so vivid and concrete that time and thought stop.

And then start again.

Some sort of impossible abyss is crossed each time we move. I sit still, pencil in hand, and then I begin to write. How does that happen? How does stillness become motion? It's the Paradox of Xeno: to move an inch, you need to first move a half an inch. But to move that half inch you first need to move a quarter inch. But first an eighth, a sixteenth and so on until we learn that motion is, in fact, impossible. And so the boy and I sat, shadows rolling gently across our faces, disdainful time passing us by.

Then, simultaneously, we looked up.

The sun was high in the sky, and all around us were children. How many? Dozens. Silent and observing, just like their sister,

Zoe. Soft shadows mottled their heads, and I saw how thin they were. Somehow I'd come to assume that these kids were otherworldly apparitions, phantoms untethered from the trials of Nod. But now I saw it wasn't true: they were as human and hungry as any child from a World Visions appeal, with eyes as large and round as those of children from velvet paintings. What had they been subsisting on for the last couple of weeks? I stretched my mind across the park. Maybe the contents of a couple of plundered refreshment stands and some muddy creek water. Blackberries and huckleberries. Not much.

The children turned as one and began to walk. My erstwhile companion hopped up and joined them, so I did too. Deeper and deeper into the woods I went, pulled along in their wake as they spread out and then ran with an amazing lightness and sureness of foot. I could barely hear a thing besides my own black bear thump as I blundered along behind them, but I saw some wonderful things.

The trees grew taller and taller while the curled ferns and spindly huckleberry bushes became greener and greener. So many different shades of green—I'd no idea. Giant cedars flung their arms out in exclamations of frozen motion. Fat mushrooms seemed to bop, mad with excitement, though safely tethered to the ground. All around us the world was doing a toddler's pee dance.

The entire afternoon was a kind of benign swarming: the children would disperse, then gather around some object of interest—a tiger lily or even a candy wrapper some jogger had dropped a month ago. They—we— would examine it then move on in a constant focussing and dilating flow. Occasionally we'd stray into a patch of berries and the children would pick and share them, hand to hand, then gulp them down, Seattle-dust and all.

As evening approached and the light began to wane, we slowed our pace. And as things slowed, a sound grew: the Ragnarok, of course.

There was a shrill new edge in its engine's upper register, a high-pitched whine that frightened me. The sound affected me like a baby's cry: an irresistible demand. And so I came back into myself, back into narrative and a sense of urgent mission.

I shook off my pack, unzipped it, and reached for the flare gun Tyler had given me. Then I grabbed the hand of the nearest child, a girl of about six, and began to march toward the sound. As though connected to one another by invisible threads, the rest of the children trailed after us.

Soon I could see the bridge tower through the trees. Its white electric lights were cold and static, but the fires raging on its deck looked warm and alive. Our path emerged onto the seawall within a couple of hundred meters from the ship's prow. The crowd's attention was focussed on the flames on the deck, and for the moment, no one saw us.

The children gathered around me, watching and blinking while I raised the gun in the air and fired. The flare arched up into the sky and exploded above us, lighting and freezing the scene. I felt thousands of eyes swivel in their sockets, could almost hear the moist sound of that movement in the same way a million silent raindrops become a deafening torrent. I prayed that Tyler was up there in his bridge keeping an eye out for my signal. I wasn't going to be able to introduce Zoe to him in time, so if anything was going to touch his heart, it was going to have to be this tableau.

On the beach, a blur of shapes began moving toward us, the nearer ones taking on human form as they spilled out of the dusk. The children did nothing, just stared at me while I stared at the horde, a football field—no, a parking lot—away.

Time for us to go. I turned and ran. The children first followed then floated past me like leaves driven by a storm, disappearing in dozens of different directions.

Eventually I stopped, exhausted and unable to hear anything over the frenzied tomtom of my heart. Then as my heart slowed I became aware of an almost total silence, but it took me a few moments to realize what that silence meant: the Ragnarok's engines had shut down. In my mind's eye, I saw Tyler loading up one last syringe, then shuffling below deck to lie down on a clean white bed for the final time.

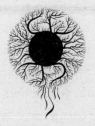

DAY 16
CONEY-CATCHING

Elizabethan slang for theft through trickery. It comes from the word 'coney' (sometimes spelled conny), meaning a rabbit raised for the table and thus tame.

I spent the rest of that night stumbling through the forest while a light rain fell, evading the disturbed hive of the Awakened but unable to make much headway toward the Yellow School and Zoe. The people scouring the woods that night weren't Charles' people, but rather the damp damned random lost souls determined to catch themselves a Sleeper. With their exhausted, shambling gaits, they were eminently avoidable as they tripped over drunken tree roots or stood, bereft of purpose, in moonlit forest clearings staring up at the invisible clouds. And so my night was a Denny's place mat—a maze game designed for bored, not-too-bright kids, traced by crayon intent. Or, to put it another way, the hunters were all blundering Elmer Fudds, and I was a bemused Bugs Bunny, munching on my metaphorical carrot as I crouched behind ferns and slid along muddy unused trails.

Eventually, though, bemusement mouldered—inevitably— into pity. I watched as an old man wrapped his arms around a tree and sobbed. I saw a young woman staggering around in circles, calling out random diminutives in the sweetest voice she could muster. Now that they were so far gone, it was somehow easier to remember that these malformed shapes had very recently been just like me.

We'd been similar like squirrels—all of us scouting out nuts for winter. Some of those nuts had been called 'money' while others had been called 'wisdom' or 'fame' or 'love', but the distinctions didn't seem important any more. The businessman scurrying around after his millions and the poetic youth looking for a warm place in the gaze of some girl or boy—I could hardly tell the difference. Like the old Eskimos and their reputed fifty words for snow, we'd had thousands of way to describe the same desperate scramble for security.

The rain stopped, the sky cleared and stars wheeled in the sky as the planet spun beneath my feet, taking me along for the ride. Together, the Earth and I turned our backs on night and were rewarded by yet another visit from the sun—a foggy, mausoleum dawn that cloaked the tops of the cedars and made everything around me appear draped in gauze.

The wanderers I encountered that morning posed no threat: their minds were as befogged as the forest itself. Just like we mistake barren trees for hostile strangers in the moonlight, so in that drowsy dawn the disoriented Awakened became trees, and I easily evaded them as they emerged then faded away into the mist, one after the other. I had the general sense that I was headed toward Lost Lagoon and the West End, or at least I thought I did. The Rabbit Hunt would be starting soon, and I had to get back to the school and free Zoe.

But it didn't work out that way.

Coming around a bend in the trail I was following, I found myself on the edge of a small, grassy clearing. And suddenly there was no need for me to seek out Zoe.

Zoe had come to me.

Standing in the centre of a misty clearing, hands behind her back, she'd been cleaned up and dressed in a freshly-laundered white frock and sandals. Spying me, Zoe's eyes lit up with recognition and she smiled, but remained put. My first impulse was to go to her, but something held me back. Perhaps it was the sheer impossibility of the scene. Or perhaps it was a sound I thought I heard, something so seashell quiet as to teeter on the edge of audibility. Whispering? Maybe.

In any event, I backed up, then crept silently into the underbrush. Concealing myself behind one of the old moss-covered stumps that littered the park, I watched and waited.

Having lost sight of me, Zoe showed no signs of concern. Instead, she looked blandly around. A barely discernible brightness above us indicated the presence of clear skies somewhere beyond the top of the canopy, but for now the park remained wrapped in its fallen cloud.

After a few minutes there was a rustling in the bush to my left and one of the children I'd run with earlier, a tall boy of about twelve, entered the clearing. Zoe's face lit up once more at the sight of him. Smiling, he began to move toward her. As he did so, another figure emerged from the fog behind Zoe. It was Gytrash, the old woman I'd left in the bookroom when I'd rescued Brandon. She was wrapped in a long navy blue cloak, wicker basket under her arm—a sight straight out of a fairy tale, back when fairy tales were fairy tales, if you know what I mean. Not Disneyfied pandering, but rather eerie cautionary tales for the young—don't-go-into-the-woods-or-a-wolf-will-shred-and-devour-you fairy tales. She was from one of those.

When the old get exhausted, you can begin to see through the surface of their translucent skin, right down to the liquid workings below. Gytrash looked as though her face had been dragged a few miles down a country lane tied to the back of a pickup truck then stapled back onto her skull. Worst of all, though, was her smile—a crude mimicry of care and grandma-welcome. The mouth that framed that ghastly smile was a black hole of greeting, stretched open so wide that her eyes were reduced to glittering pinpricks. She was a witch, just as surely as the creatures on the beach a few nights earlier had been scorpions and crows.

But the boy didn't notice any of this. Catching sight of the crone, he paused in his advance toward Zoe but didn't turn and run. Rather he froze just as a deer does when coming across a human being—as a prelude to flight. For her part, Gytrash slowly removed the basket from her arm, then awkwardly knelt and laid it on the damp grass.

Nodding encouragingly, mouth still open wide, she began removing a selection of goodies from the basket—cookies, juice boxes, a couple of bruised apples—and laying them down on the ground in a neat line, without ever taking her eyes off the boy.

She held up an apple, nodding encouragement. The boy didn't move, but his eyes flickered back and forth between Zoe and the food and you could see he was famished. His instincts said no, but Zoe's proximity to the old woman said yes. Noticing this, Gytrash reached back into the basket and pulled out, of all things, the stuffed grizzly. She made a point of handing it to Zoe, who glowed at the sight. Taking the bear into her arms, she held it to her chest and rocked it slowly.

The boy smiled, and this tilted the scales. He began to advance toward the proffered apple.

'That's right, that's right...' Gytrash said.

When he was about three feet from the basket, all hell broke loose. Three men, their faces painted bright yellow, leapt from the underbrush and threw themselves at the boy. Zoe turned and tried to run, but fell to the ground. That was when I saw the rope around her right ankle. She was tethered to a stake driven into the ground.

As the yellow-faced men threw the boy down, Gytrash staggered to her feet and began to dance around them, shrieking, 'Tie him! Tie him!'

The men did just that, binding the child's hands and feet

then standing back, panting, to regard their work.

'Got him!' a balding man with long stringy hair cried joyously. The yellow paint that caked his face had also covered his hair, slicking it back into a plastic mane. 'Tell the Admiral we got another one!'

'Shhh,' another hissed. 'No loud noises!'

The man who'd yelled dropped his chin down onto his chest as two other yellow-painted men emerged from the fog carrying the sort of staves I'd seen being assembled in the basement.

'Look at the freak.' One of the new arrivals sneered, stabbing the point of his weapon into the boy's side. Blood began to flow freely from the wound, and the boy screamed silently, terror roiling across his agonized features. The silence made it worse: suffering without the catharsis of sound is a terrible thing to behold.

Gytrash, meanwhile, crept forward and dipped her fingers into the blood flowing from the wound. Then she lifted her fingers toward her mouth, tongue flicking, only to have her hand knocked away by the balding man's stave.

'No demon blood for the Awakened! You don't want that shit in you.'

She glared at him furiously, but wiped her fingers on the grass and shuffled away.

'Take him and put him with the others,' the man said, and he and his compatriots dragged the writhing boy off into the fog while the old woman repacked her basket and followed them.

Zoe was alone again, and it was like nothing had happened. She picked herself up off the ground and stood in roughly the same spot as before, her face devoid of expression, the grizzly hanging limp from her hand. She looked toward the trail where she'd seen me disappear and stared for a long while. Then she turned away.

The Rabbit Hunt had begun.

My only thought now was how to free Zoe. The obvious option was to walk into the clearing and try to bullshit my way into having the yellow men set Zoe free, but I was pretty sure that my currency as Charles' pet prophet had collapsed completely during the last twenty four hours and that such a move would be tantamount to suicide. Beyond that, all I had was the pack that Tyler had given me back on the Ragnarok.

I emptied it. Two items foregrounded themselves immediately: a folding knife and the flare gun I'd used to signal the Ragnarok the night before. A knife to cut the rope that bound Zoe's ankle and the flare gun to hopefully scare the shit out of the Grimm brothers and their wicked witch. I reloaded as silently as I could, though every creak of my bones and click of the gun's cartridge holder seemed amplified by the wet air.

As the day warmed, the fog was beginning to melt like cotton candy in the mouth. Already wispy, it would soon be gone completely along with whatever cover it had offered. There was no time to lose.

I pointed the gun at the underbrush behind Zoe where Charles' people had disappeared, closed my eyes, and squeezed the trigger. The effect was immediate and impressive. A loud whoosh was instantly followed by a neon pink explosion as the flare hit the ground and burst into fizzling chemical fire, sending up plumes of white, acrid smoke. Screams rang out as I sprinted forward. Falling literally at Zoe's feet, knife in hand, I sawed frantically at the nylon cord that bound her thin ankle. It wasn't easy: the knife was sharp but not serrated—unsuited for this kind of task.

Then the severed rope fell to the ground, and she was free. I leapt to my feet, took her hand, and we sprinted out of the clearing just as her erstwhile captors entered it, Gytrash at their rear, urging them on.

As we ran, the fog continued to thin. We were nearing the edge of the woods and the grass playing fields that lay beyond them, perhaps a half kilometre from Lagoon Drive. From there, it was only a couple of blocks further to Tanya's and my old apartment, the only place I could conjure up as a possible destination.

But then, directly ahead of us, I saw something I'll never forget.

Charles' Thousand, swarming over an old stone bridge on the west side of Lost Lagoon, straight toward us. Staves in hand, they were spreading out into a large playing field in preparation for their march into the woods. And their heads, all of them, were painted bright yellow.

From this distance they didn't seem to have faces. Rather, their bodies appeared to be topped by sticky, shiny blobs. Lollipop soldiers. Here and there among them were children from the park tethered to ropes. Bait, like Zoe had been.

We were still just inside the woods' shadow, so they couldn't see us yet, but there was no way we were going to be able to pass through that yellow line, and there was nothing behind us but woods, more woods, and then the churning ocean. I thought of trying to make it back to the dinghy, but I had no idea of what path to take, never mind that I was out of flares and Tyler was almost certainly dead. And so, no sooner had Zoe and I leapt out of one frying pan than we landed splat in the centre of another.

The crowd parted and a figure came forward over the crest of the bridge. There was no mistaking the Admiral of the Blue, even at that distance: his face and clothing were the same blazing hue as the summer sky. He spread his arms wide, shouting orders as his Thousand spread left and right, their line widening. Then Charles did something unexpected. He stopped his shouting and stared.

Straight at Zoe and me.

There was no way he could have seen us, wrapped as we were in shadow and the last wisps of the morning's fog—but somehow he must have sensed that somebody was out there watching him. And that feeling stopped him dead in his tracks. I was too far away to see the expression on his face, to see anything but a mad slash of blue. Still, I braced myself, waiting for him to cry out and send death and destruction flying in our direction.

But that's not what happened.

Instead, Charles' head snapped around to look back over the bridge he'd just crossed.

Then I heard a new sound—the unmistakable roar of car engines, so strange and so familiar. It could only mean one thing: London's Cat Sleepers had arrived.

Shots rang out and the Thousand began to force their way back across the bridge, urged on by Charles' frantic figure. Taking advantage of the pandemonium on the field, Zoe and I ran north around Lost Lagoon. The hard-packed gravel path was abandoned, and within a couple of minutes we were on the city side and circling back toward what was by now the scene of a pitched battle.

London's people had arrived on the scene in a dozen SUVs, their path through downtown's obstacle course having been blazed by a pair of snowploughs that now sat abandoned on the side of the street. The SUVs were lined up at the edge of the park, with the Cat Sleepers in their white T-shirts and khakis crouched behind the vehicles' opened doors, sniping at the Awakened as they advanced. There were no more than fifty or sixty of them, but they were all armed to the teeth, so it was far from a fair battle. In fact, it was shaping up to be a massacre. You could almost keep count as the bodies fell one after another: 1000, 999, 998, 997...

Then another strange-familiar sound. I looked up and saw a helicopter descending from the now clear sky. It hovered twenty feet above the ground as riflemen shot casually and precisely down into Charles' Rabbit Hunters. The Awakened were now officially fucked. They ran at the conglomeration of SUVs in waves of ten or twenty, only to be mowed down each time they tried. The bodies of perhaps two hundred of them already littered the path.

'At the same time! Attack them at the same time!!' Charles screamed from the rear.

The remaining Awakened hurled themselves at the row of SUVs, a wave of yellow. The Cat Sleepers held their positions, though, and increased the tempo of their firing as the helicopter hovered over the scene.

Charles watched the battle unfold, clenching and unclenching his hands. Then he looked up once more. This time he saw us. A look of intense hatred possessed his features. Unable to form words, he howled, a crazed sound that seemed to intensify the fighting like lightning seems to intensify a rain storm.

By now, a few of the Awakened had reached the nearest SUV and rammed their staves through the open windows into the bodies of shooters who'd paused to reload. Shaken, the other Cat Sleepers abandoned their positions and began to fire on the run, seeking cover behind trees and other vehicles parked on the street. The line was broken, but Charles' people were still falling by the dozen as the gunmen in the helicopter kept firing.

And so Zoe and I made our way home. That's what you do when you run out of options: you go home. Ask a failed college student or a new mother whose partner disappears. Ask the parolee and the schizophrenic. No matter what home is. Even if home is a false hope. You just pick yourself up and go there. Then you sit down and wait to see what happens next.

The old apartment building was in no better or worse shape than any other. Broken glass outside and the sweet smell of decomposition within. We climbed the dark stairs then locked ourselves inside the apartment, which looked much the same as it had ever done, despite having been looted in a desultory fashion during our absence.

I went out on the balcony. There wasn't much to see, though there was plenty to hear. Shots and screams echoed back and forth through the trees, rising and falling like the ocean's swell. I went back inside.

There was no radio to turn on to drown out the sounds. All I could do was close the balcony doors and the windows and wait for it to be over.

It was hard to remain awake. My eyes burned with everything I'd seen and done. I played a game of hide and seek with Zoe and the grizzly; I pinched myself and bit my lips, just as Tanya had done two weeks earlier.

In the late afternoon, I put Zoe to bed, closing the blinds in the bedroom as tightly as I could, then sat on the couch in the living room thinking about what to do next. If he'd survived the rout in the park, Charles would be coming after us very soon, and this would be the first place he'd look.

The time was drawing very near when the Awakened would no longer present any sort of threat to Zoe and she would be free to go—and I would be free to sleep. But what to do in the interim?

There was no way to fortify the ground level which was, typically for Vancouver, made mostly of glass. So I did the only thing I could think of and spent the night throwing furniture down the stairwell's gullet. It felt a lot like madness, but an enjoyable madness. I went down to the second floor and began to drag chairs, tables, exercise bikes, cappuccino machines, and even some of the lighter couches out of the apartments and down the hall in order to pitch them into that black hole. I worked like a devil in the sweltering darkness, laughing to myself, at myself, stripped to the waist and dripping with sweat. It was about the best time I'd had since the world ended. My body felt wonderfully used and my mind was clear to the point of transparency.

When the stairwell was filled to the second level, I climbed up and jumped up and down on that contortion of *stuff*, cramming it as tightly as I could. Then I climbed up to the third floor and repeated the process. Now, however, I began to approach my task as a kind of jigsaw puzzle, figuring out how best to jam this chair against that chest of drawers or this guitar into that microwave oven. I imagined Charles' people trying to untangle the mess and laughed some more.

By the time the sun rose, I'd filled the stairwell up to the fourth floor. Sliding down the nearest wall, my muscles burning, I laughed and cried. Nod was almost over. My final stand had begun.

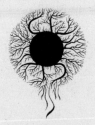

DAY 17
CHURCHYARD COUGH

A consumptive cough, indicating the approach of death.

As the next day began, the skyscrapers began to direct their long shadows toward the park, pointing accusingly toward the wreckage of the Rabbit Hunt. The streets were utterly quiet, except for the familiar whoomph of herons landing and taking off from the cedars across the way. They'd launch themselves and disappear, but the bough they'd abandoned would bounce up and down in slow motion for a good thirty seconds longer.

The way I saw it, the longest Zoe and I would have to survive up here would be a week before the remaining Awakened were either dead or completely incapacitated. In the meantime, I was pretty sure I could scavenge enough food from the building to keep us going. In fact, I'd already managed to secure a few cans of lonelyhearts food: kippers, asparagus, and water chestnuts. Yellow label stuff mostly. Even demented foragers had their standards.

In order to last the week, though, the main thing we'd need would be water, and I had a theory that I was eager to try out. When I envisioned the building's water supply, I pictured an incredibly intricate three dimensional grid—a completely sealed unit. But it couldn't be a perfect grid: there had to be slopes and sags. And if this was so, there would be water trapped in the lines at various points; flat runs of copper behind walls and inside ceilings that previous scavengers would almost certainly have missed.

With this in mind, I found a hacksaw and set to work kicking in the drywall behind sinks, tubs, and toilets. I'd hack through copper tubing and direct the severed ends toward a plastic bucket I'd found. And it worked. Not a lot came out, just a trickle here and a trickle there, but by noon I had almost two litres of metallic-tasting but clean water for Zoe and me to drink. I felt like the most resourceful guy in Vancouver and—given the nature of the competition—I probably was.

Back in the apartment we ate lunch: cold mushroom soup with crackers and stale water. It was a silent meal, needless to say. Zoe fed the grizzly crackers (it was a messy eater) with her typical attention and contentment.

As I watched her, I wondered what would become of these children when we were gone. Would they grow up into mute adults and, in turn, have mute babies of their own? If I'm to be honest, part of me recoiled slightly at the thought of a planet populated by Zoe's kind. The thought of a universally-benign species taking over the planetary reins seemed like a kind of cheat, seemed pointless. What about struggle? What about confusion and turmoil? All those tried and true character builders? What about words?

But if I'm forced to hazard a guess, Zoe and her friends are probably just some sort of next step in evolution. In that case, I'm one of the throwbacks and my opinion doesn't count any more than that of a Neanderthal surveyed about the potential of stone wheels or harnessed fire. Ug.

After we finished our lunch, I went out on the balcony and saw, as I'd expected, Charles.

He was standing on the sidewalk glaring up at me. Around him were gathered what was probably the last ten of his yellow-faced Thousand. Zoe appeared beside me, her chubby hands clutching the iron rails of the balcony like the world's tiniest jailbird.

Watching Charles' trembling face turned up at me, I thought of something my father had said a few years back about his cancer diagnosis and the anticlimactic tumour that had failed to kill him. He said the worst thing about having cancer was that nothing really changed. You were still you, even in the middle of that potentially-life-ending drama. The phone calls and tinfoil-wrapped lasagnes lasted for a few days or a week, then they stopped and you were just lumped with cancer like you were lumped with a job or a mortgage or a second-rate marriage. That, he felt, was the disease's most terrible secret: not the suffering it prompted, not the death it dealt in, but its ultimate mundanity. Well, that afternoon Charles looked as though his body housed a cancer too phlegmatic to finish him off. And he looked as though he'd been trying to scratch the cancer out of himself with his fingernails for decades. Nod was nothing new to Charles—it was an old and bitter dream. In the end, it wasn't some sort of monster that stared silently up at me until night fell and he crept away, but an ordinary man. And that was the most terrifying thing I ever saw in Nod: humanity.

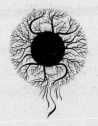

DAYS 19-22
ROUGH MUSIC

*A ceremony which takes place after sunset, when performers,
to show their indignation against some man or woman who
has outraged propriety, assemble before the house and make an
appalling din with bells, horns, tin plates, and other
noisy instruments.*

I'm writing purely to keep myself awake now. I began this journal three or so days ago and have been scribbling constantly when not hunting for water and food for Zoe. And finally I find myself here in the present tense. The action tank is dry, and what follows will be strictly denouement—I hope.

It's not quite safe to let Zoe go yet, though the pull to sleep is almost overwhelming. A couple of times each day I almost lose it, almost become a complete stranger to myself and drift away once and for all. Then I think of Zoe and slowly ease myself back down into myself, a ghost wiggling back into its former body through a hole in the top of the head, gripping the ears for traction. But it's getting harder.

Ever since the Rabbit Hunt went south, there's been a lot of activity around the base of my apartment. Charles and his remaining followers keep trying to burn the building down. It's kind of funny, actually. In all fairness, though, it's hard to burn down a concrete building—even when one is in full possession of one's wits.

Each day at nightfall, Charles crawls up onto a pathetic stage they've built and makes some sort of rambling, increasingly incoherent speech about the Ragnarok taking him home, about my evil nature, and about the beast I am supposed to be harbouring up here in my tower of darkness. Then he collapses and twitches like a trout in the belly of a boat. An hour or four pass and then he staggers to his swollen, curled feet and froths some more. After that he and the two or three who still follow him around go and set some half-assed fire in the lobby. I hear giggling, then growling, then sobbing.

Last night, though, their efforts almost came to something. I heard crackling and smelled smoke, but concrete construction foiled them yet again. Still, for a while, it must have been exciting. When they're not setting fires, they try to untangle the jammed stairwells or worm their way up into the ceilings. But so far, so good.

Earlier this evening, while Zoe played with her bear, I snuck down to the fourth floor. Leaning out of a window directly above the stage, I called Charles' name. He looked up and smiled faintly, clawing with blind hands in my general direction. Poor Charles. Never sleeping means that he is ceaselessly himself—and the honest-to-Bosch truth is that that has to be a good working definition of Hell. Not just to be Charles all the time, but to be any of us.

'Paul? Is that you? Come out to play, Paul!'

'How are you doing, Charles?'

'I'm a king, Paul! Nod is mine!'

'Well, you're welcome to it.'

'I saw you, you know. Before! I saw you step over some smelly drunk on the sidewalk one day. Was he sleeping? Was he dead? You didn't care! You didn't see him, Paul! To see anything you'd have had to stay awake for days, right? But I saw things all the time. There'd be a pretty couple in the park, breaking up. Then the next day I see lover boy and there are bags under his eyes. So I pay attention and watch him making his rounds for the next few days—to work, to Starbucks, to Safeway, and home. Maybe to the bank. I watch the bags under his eyes get deeper. Then I know he's seeing something. Maybe he even looks at *me* for a second when he walks past. He starts to see me! But then something scares him, and he scurries away. Then what? A week later I see him reading a newspaper, and he's been put back together. Magic! He did it with drinks or dope or some fresh pussy, or I don't know what. Then he doesn't see me anymore. He doesn't see anything.'

'I don't know what to say, Charles. I'm sorry if your life was hard. But it was hard for a lot of people.'

'Why don't you come down here, Paul? Come visit old Charles.'

'You know I can't do that. I've got to take care of the child.'

Suddenly, he is in a frenzy, writhing on his stage, trying but unable to stand.

'Protecting the child? Why? Innocence is just torture delayed. And torture delayed is just worse torture!'

And then he was on his knees, weeping. After a few minutes, slowly, agonizingly, he crawled to the edge of his stage, fell to the ground with a thud, and slithered out of sight. No more danger. No more plans. No more followers. No more Nod. That was the last time I ever saw him.

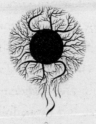

DAY 24
HOT COCKLES

A Christmas game. One blindfolded knelt down, and
being struck had to guess who gave the blow.

Every day is important; each day makes us. Even the nothing ones—*especially* those, given how they silt up, slowly burying other, seemingly more momentous, moments beneath their weight. I see that now.

What we used to blithely call 'wasting time' was actually a euphemism for the tenement architecture of our lives; there wasn't an ounce of waste in a ton of those lost hours. Proof of this could be seen in the fact that even as we imagined we were killing time with movies and phone calls, careers and frozen pizzas, time was slowly but surely killing us. But who knew? It may not end up being a compelling defence to have to make before a ticked-off Jesus come Judgement Day (quite

possibly today, now that I think about it), but still it's true—
who knew?

In these final hours, I meditate on the passing of Nod and—
of course—on words. There's more power in words than
people think. How does the Bible begin? *In the beginning was
the Word.* Nod was the miracle of the undergraduate poet, the
sensitive young person who discovers that he or she can combine
adjectives and nouns higgledy piggledy and come up with all
sorts of fantastic monsters: cowering towers, fierce slumber,
panicky taxis, shy murderers, and the like.

During my time in Nod, I came to believe that if
something can be imagined it must be possible. Want proof?
We imagined space flight, then it happened for real. We
imagined holograms and they happened too. We imagined
teleportation and just a couple of summers ago I read how
some Australian scientists teleported a beam of light an inch
or two. So is a Rice Christian or a Blemmye or a burning
ice cube or a green sun or a widowed scarecrow just some
meaningless assemblage of sounds and letters? Or, in some
way, are they all real? Wow, I'm really babbling here in
Babylon, holed up in my tower of words.

What would it be like to be an animal in that cold frontier
beyond words? A grizzly pacing out infinite forest? A blind
crustacean at the bottom of a frigid black sea? To see *without*
words, to emerge from words' insect haze and breathe only air?

I can't tell you what it's like. Instead, you get all this. Words,

words, words. Meaning swishing slowly back and forth like the tail of a hackling dog, menacing centuries. Nod.

I lower Zoe from the fourth floor. In a basket, on a rope. She lands gently on the sidewalk, untangles herself, then runs off toward the park without looking back, grizzly dangling. Goodbye again, Tanya.

So this is my final entry. Time to say goodbye to it all, to the world and all of the words I've loved so much. Goodbye to it all.

I go to my bed and lie down flat on my back.

Goodbye to chocolate and puppies and hard ons and old running shoes and used books and Christmas morning and crisp newspapers and babies and Coca Cola and sunburned skin on white cotton sheets and bad moods and late night eating and high speed Internet and Charlie Brown and ice cream and Beatle music and Beach Boy harmonies and fruit smoothies and thrift stores and black and white photos and favourite books and cold beer and snow storms and heavy rain and meals in restaurants and arriving and departing and exhaustion and the need to piss and tiredness and bicycles and cars and kisses on the neck and stretching and arguments and water and salt and paintings and shade and Dickensian waifs and waxy pine needles and hot sand and the smell of cedar and every line Shakespeare ever wrote and shaving and sore muscles and crunching ice cubes and mail boxes and popcorn in movie theatres and pay cheques and the smell of limes and

AUTHOR'S NOTE

My Cancer is as Strange as my Fiction

Six months ago I was discovered to have the tumor Glioblastoma Multiforme living inside my skull. At the same time my new novel *Nod* was approaching publication in North America. As both the disease and my novel progressed I began to notice eerie similarities between the two, even down to the physical similarity between the eye on the book's cover and an image of the tumor itself, with its vein-like tendrils spreading out across my brain.

Glioblastoma Multiforme, alas, is the most fatal of all cancers and is known to have a death rate of about 99%. In terms of the amount of life left, the average is one year. The really horrible part is the torturous treatment period of six months. Throughout the last six months I have had toxic drugs pumped into me. My skull has been cut open and cuts have been made at both my brain and the tumor itself. My optic nerve has been severed and I've been assaulted by radiation. On and on. All this, not to cure us, but to buy us the second six months.

There are around 75,000 North Americans with the same form of cancer, if you can imagine. I can't quite. Divide it by 50 states and then try to imagine 3,000 people in each state, blending in, so to speak. And this among all the various forms of cancer out there in massively large numbers. It's astounding.

I have lost my career as a college teacher, my work as owner of a local news company, and my ability to both read and write. I've also lost the most important part of life: music. I've lost the sounds, lost the lyrics, and lost both the songs and lyrics that I used to write. Not a single song is left.

At the same time this has been happening, my latest novel, *Nod*, is due for publication any day now. And this is where the story gets weird.

The concept of *Nod* came to me as a sort of dream and fascination I have always had with life and death and how they intertwine. When I wrote the novel I wanted to explore what happens when the world ends while some of us watch it with our eyes painfully open (hence the cover). In my novel, the sun comes one day and almost no one has slept a wink. Only a small few have not lost the ability to sleep, one of them is my character Paul.

Retaining his sanity through sleep, Paul has to watch the horror and insanity that occurs when insomnia rules the world. He watches everything he's known be slowly destroyed, his partner included, sleepless at his side.

And so the similarities between Paul and I emerge.

Since then, I began to see the end of everything. I was going to slowly lose the people I love, as did Paul. Insomnia made the world insane to Paul just as my damaged brain has made the world insane to me.

And this is only beginning of the weird similarities.

I'm not traditionally religious, but I've always been fascinated by all religions and learned a lot from the Bible's Book of Job. In that famous story God and Satan have a conversation about human beings. Satan says he can ruin them all, but God says he can't destroy the good Job and gives Satan free rein to break the man.

And so Satan destroys Job's property, his family, and his body, trying to make Job despair and hate God. But Job pulls himself together and keeps his faith until the end. It's quite a chapter if you don't know it.

And so the first lines of *Nod* were these words quoted from Book of Job:

And Cain went out from the face of the Lord and
dwelt in the land Nod on the east syde of Eden

God and I both put Job and Paul literally into Hell. To see what? What's left, I suppose, when everything is taken from us. But the joke was on me because the loss of everything was now done to me as well. Why? Well, that's the question, isn't it? I think I wanted to know—and still want to know—what is essential in this world. Well, I do understand now that my novel and my life have made the same journey.

Perhaps the strangest similarity between life and *Nod* lies in the fact that Paul ends up in the Vancouver Hospital seeking help. It's now the same place where I go to for my surgery and drugs. Paul witnessed a room full of the tortured in *Nod* and I, my fellow patients in the cancer ward.

As the places of *Nod* grow stranger, so too do my eyes as I see things through the delusions of my drugs. And I finished the book a whole year before my health fell apart.

Today I kind of see my situation as a sort of battle between Me and My Tumour. Which of us will win and which of us will die.

Looking back at my life before all this, and even before I wrote *Nod*, I think I despaired the human species and thus wrote a fairly tough, dramatic novel in *Nod*. I often cursed the real world, with its greed and hatred and the lack of love. The rich were worshiped while the poor were ignored. All true, all I still believe.

But the great gift I've received from my tumor is the answers to these fears about Earth. As my thinking and worrying fell apart over the last six months, when all my strengths dissolved, what was left was love. The love I feel for my people and the love I feel coming from them.

As for Paul, well, I drove him through the Hell of his world dying but I am so grateful that, in the very last moment of the novel, I left him with peace and the dream of hope.

Through all of this I've learned what is important and what isn't. Somewhere in my mind I must have known all this, but now I know it in my life. And I think it's all that matters. If

I'd lived another 20 years not seeing the point of love, I'd have wasted years, probably avoiding death as I wasted life. But now I get half a year, or so, to truly live. So how can I resent or mourn things as they are?

And I'm grateful about it all, weird as that may sound. God allowed Job to be put through Hell and he came out the other end as a joyful man. I think God has done the same for me and I find that love does overcome life.

It's been such a weird story to share with you.

Due to my damaged memory, I couldn't recall the end of *Nod* so I went back and checked. I was relieved to see that I'd given Paul some peace just as I've received some myself. *Phew*, I thought, because, let me tell you, I was less than kind to the world as a whole.

And so I sit here this morning. I live in my old home, Rossland, British Columbia. We live in the mountains and right now, as in so many places, a giant fire is only six miles from outside our front doors. With the wrong gust of wind our world will burn and descend into chaos. How's that for yet another similarity with *Nod*?

This massive fire burns as I type away this moment, with cancer and *Nod* right beside me. The city council has told us all to be ready to run. If the winds change all 3,000 of us may have to run. But it's okay. Love will save us all, even if our houses burn to the ground.

Adrian Barnes
Originally published in *The Daily Beast*, October 2015

ABOUT THE AUTHOR

Adrian Barnes was born in Blackpool, England and moved to Vancouver, Canada in 1969. He and his former wife, Charlene, raised their two sons, Ethan and Liam in Rossland, BC. He received a MA in Creative Writing from Manchester Metropolitan University and *Nod* is his first published novel.